Rashad took her han

through the groups touring the street.

She was leading, and he didn't want to lose her, but it felt good to have her hand for other reasons, too. She looked back at him and smiled, plunging them along through the crowd.

"Does this place ever quiet down?" he asked once they made it to the restaurant.

"I've been at Regina's shop until midnight, and there were still people in the streets," Michelle said.

"That's right. Did we pass it?"

"Yes, but I can point it out on the way back, when we have more time."

The restaurant was still open, and they were seated right away.

Rashad took Michelle's hands in his while they waited for their late-night meal. He saw her get still and quiet, but she didn't take her hand away. Instead, she smiled at him.

"I like the feel of your hands," she said. "They're strong."

"Yours are soft. I like that, too."

Books by Yasmin Sullivan

Harlequin Kimani Romance

Return to Love
Love on the High Seas
In His Arms

YASMIN SULLIVAN

grew up in upstate New York and St. Thomas, Virgin Islands, from which her family hails. She moved to Washington, D.C., to attend college and has earned degrees from Howard University and Yale University. As an academic writer, she has published on works by Frederick Douglass, Harriet Jacobs, James Baldwin, Maya Angelou and Ed Bullins, as well as the writing of the Negritude Movement and historical fiction treating emancipation in the Danish West Indies/United States Virgin Islands. She currently lives in Washington, D.C., where she teaches with a focus on African-American and Caribbean literatures. When she is not teaching, she also does creative writing and works on mosaics.

in His ARMS
YASMIN SULLIVAN
HARLEQUIN® KIMANI™ ROMANCE

If you purchased this book without a cover you should be aware that this book is stolen property. It was reported as "unsold and destroyed" to the publisher, and neither the author nor the publisher has received any payment for this "stripped book."

For my mother, father, brother and grandmother,
who have given me the richness of the human heart;
for Jennie and Tanya,
who have been my sister-friends;
for Madeline, Freddie and William,
who have shaped my vision of love;
and for Vionette and Lois,
who have inspired the romantic in me.

Recycling programs for this product may not exist in your area.

ISBN-13: 978-0-373-86339-6

IN HIS ARMS

For questions and comments about the quality of this book please contact us at CustomerService@Harlequin.com.

Printed in U.S.A.

Dear Reader,

In Zora Neale Hurston's *Their Eyes Were Watching God,* Tea Cake, Janie's third husband, reminds her to be young and enjoy life. Tea Cake's sentiments should inspire us to embrace laughter in our lives and to capture life before it is gone.

This novel is the story of Michelle Johns and Rashad Brown, who can find laughter and life only if they both let go of the past—either its heartaches or expectations.

I am so glad that you have decided to share their love story with me. I am already at work on my next romance project, but for now, I would love to hear your thoughts on this book. Please write me at yasminhu@aol.com.

Warm wishes,

Yasmin

Chapter 1

Michelle Johns sat at her dining table with her schoolwork in front of her and her son in the chair next to her. Her little one had been quiet for a while. Michelle tipped her head, glanced at him out of the corner of her eye and smiled.

For the past hour, he had been turning pages in his storybook as she turned pages in her communications law book. Andre was just beginning to learn how to read simple words, and the book he had was one that she read to him at bedtime—one with lots of words to go with the pictures.

Nevertheless, he was intent on their task and peered at the pages before him.

Andre was just beginning to grow out of his baby fat and acquire the spindly limbs of childhood, but he still had full brown eyes with thick lashes and big round cheeks that puffed up when he smiled. His features still held the amazement of a child and the vulnerability of youth. Right now, his eyebrows were furrowed in inquiry, and the serious expression on his face ended in a little pucker on his lips that pulled at Michelle's heart.

Michelle turned to her son, wrapped her arms around him and proceeded to tickle him until they were both laughing. When they were done, she ruffled his hair and pulled him up from his chair and into her arms for a tight squeeze.

"Reading is hard work, huh?"

Andre nodded his head. "Is it time for a snack yet?"

Michelle laughed. "A snack? You just had dinner. It's time to get ready to go to the sitter so that I can get to my art class. You can have your snack over there."

"What do I get?"

"What would you like?"

Andre shrugged.

Michelle closed her book and pushed it farther onto the dining table. "You go find a couple of movies and put some of your toys and games in your knapsack, and I'll make you something for later."

Michelle put Andre's evening snack in a brown paper bag and checked on him to help pick out two movies and some toys. Then she went into her room to get clothes out for work the next day and pack her book bag for her classes tomorrow. She would be getting home a bit late, so there might not be time later on.

"Come, little one. No, first to the bathroom."

"I don't have to go now."

"Go anyway. And, actually, so should I."

When they were ready, Michelle helped Andre get his knapsack on, handed him the paper bag with his snack, grabbed the things for her art class, hustled them out the front door and walked Andre down two doors to Mrs. Miller, their neighbor and sitter.

Her class was at the Art League School in Virginia.

She had given herself some extra time to figure out a new Metro route, but since it was rush hour, she didn't wait long for the bus, and it was actually a straight shot on the yellow line from Greenbelt to King Street, where she got on the free King Street Trolley.

With her destination in sight, Michelle hopped off the trolley and strode through the crowded streets of Old Town Alexandria toward the Torpedo Factory Art Center. She couldn't suppress her excitement over the class she was starting and hurried through the milling people with her purse slung over her shoulder, her portfolio under one arm and a satchel with the required art supplies in her other hand.

She already had a lot on her plate, and this would add more, but this was her passion. It would give her the edge she knew she needed so that she could build a real future for herself and her son. She hated being away from Andre during the evenings, but it was one night a week, and it was part of their combined future. She was raising a son, getting a college degree, working full-time and now this. But she was determined to make it all work.

Michelle shook her head to clear her thoughts. It never paid off when she tried to think of everything at once; this just overwhelmed her. And she was too excited about her class to let that happen.

As she crossed North Union Street to enter the Torpedo Factory, she could see the waterfront in the background with groups of pedestrians walking the promenade. She envied their leisure, but only for a second.

A man crossed the street toward her and winked at her. Michelle put her free hand on her hip and gave him a forbidding expression. Then she winked back and laughed. He turned his head back to look at her, probably doubting her sanity, but Michelle didn't care.

She glanced at her watch and hurried inside to find her classroom.

Other students were already getting situated, and Michelle picked her way through the rows of drafting tables to find an empty one. She found one in the center of the room, propped her portfolio on the slanted desktop and began unpacking her supplies.

"First class here at the Art League?"

It was a smooth, masculine voice coming from the chair next to hers, and it seemed directed at her. She answered as she was hooking her purse on the back of her chair. "Yes. Can you tell?" She chuckled at herself for being so obvious.

When Michelle finally turned toward the voice, she found a pair of dark brown eyes gazing at her intently. They were set in an inquisitive expression on a handsome ebony face. The angular jawline held a mouth with full, soft lips, and it was smiling.

"No, you seem ready to go. It's my first class here, as well. I'm Rashad."

He offered his hand.

Michelle didn't realize that she was holding her breath until she opened her mouth to talk. She let go of a deep breath and laughed at herself.

"Hi."

"What's funny?"

"Nothing. I just amused myself." She waved her hand to dispel the thought.

"I'm glad to see another African American face in the class."

"Hmm." Michelle glanced about. There were a couple of others, but not many. "I hadn't noticed before. So am I."

"Can I ask your name?"

"I'm Michelle."

She took his outstretched hand, and a shiver ran up her arm and down her spine.

"Nice to meet you," he said.

"Same here."

Now that her supplies were unpacked, Michelle could give her full attention to the captivating figure sitting next to her. He had on a simple white dress shirt and black slacks, but she recognized the quality of the garments; they weren't cheap. The shirt, creased from a day of being worn, didn't hide the broad shoulders and muscled arms beneath it. And though he was leaning back in his chair at ease, his slacks didn't fully hide the sculpted thighs they covered. Michelle took a breath and hoped he hadn't caught her checking him out.

"Are you an artist already?" he asked.

"Not yet, but I—"

A voice interrupted her from the front of the room. The teacher for the class had just come in. "Welcome to Composition and Design Fundamentals."

Rashad nodded at Michelle, and both turned their attention to the instructor.

For the first half hour, they got an overview of what they would be learning and doing that term. Then, after brief introductions, they were given their first set of vocabulary words and their first lesson in controlling movement within a picture. They then had an hour to create their own examples before they went on to the second lesson. Though the class was three and a half hours, the amount of information packed in it and the variety of exercises they did made the time sprint by.

Still, Michelle couldn't help noticing her new acquaintance in the neighboring seat. Rashad took the class seriously, jotting down notes just as she did and concentrating on the abstract exercises that they were given. Periodically, he looked toward her and found her glancing his way. Each time she felt she had been caught in the act of ogling him, but each time he just smiled—the sweetest smile she'd ever seen—and went back to his task. It made Michelle smile, too.

For the last half hour, they got their final lesson and their homework. Then they were dismissed. People started to rustle, and some went up to the instructor with questions.

"Wow," Rashad said. "That class went by like lightning."

"I know," Michelle responded. "And it was intense all the way through."

"I know I'm going to get more than I expected out of this, which is great, considering the price."

"I know. We have nine sessions of this, and it was under two hundred dollars."

"Except for the supplies."

Michelle had closed her portfolio and was packing her supplies in her satchel. When she finished, she riffled through her purse for her Metro card, which slipped from her hand when she moved to put it into her pocket.

Before Michelle could stoop to retrieve her pass, Rashad stepped around his chair, scooped it up and held it up for her.

"Thank you," Michelle said.

"Hey, are you taking the Metro? I can give you a ride home."

"Oh, I'm not nearby. I live in Greenbelt."

"That's okay. I'm on New Hampshire Avenue near East West Highway."

Michelle gave him a puzzled look, and Rashad laughed.

"You have no idea what I'm talking about."

"None. I know that Metro map, and that's it."

Both of them laughed.

"I'm in Maryland, too," he said. "Right between Takoma Park and Silver Spring."

"Hey. I got that!"

"So let me give you a ride home."

Michelle wasn't used to taking rides from strangers and gave Rashad a hard look.

"The trolley stops at ten," he said. "So you've missed it and will have to walk to the Metro."

Michelle looked down at her shoes; they were comfortable flats, so she could do the walk.

"You're on the way for me."

Michelle finally let her guard down and smiled. "Okay. That's really, really nice of you. And," she added, "I need to get home to my son."

That usually put a halt to any interest a guy showed in her, just in case Rashad was showing interest. And she did need to get home to her son.

Actually, she said it more for herself than for him. She needed to put the possibility out of her mind because he had the most sensuous eyes she'd ever seen and looked as good as all get-out. But he didn't seem to be hitting on her, so she might as well put the possibility out of reach. And she did want to know someone else in the class.

Chapter 2

Rashad Brown slipped the extra portfolio under his arm and followed Michelle to the elevator. He would have offered to take anyone home, but he was intrigued by this woman and wanted to know more about her. There was something about how easily she smiled and how open she was that let him know he would enjoy spending time with her. He couldn't help being a little disappointed that she was taken already; son generally meant husband, as well. But she could still be a friend.

Now that class was over, he could actually look at her. She was tall, only a few inches shorter than he was, and her hair was long and loose, with a slight curl at the end. She had on a powder-blue top with lace around the neck, down the front, at the bottom of the sleeves and at the hem. It gave her a feminine quality that matched her smile. She also had on blue leggings that fit her curves in all the right places—at least as far as he could see. There was nothing fancy, but it all made her look beautiful.

When she turned around in the back of the elevator, he could see her face again. Her full cheeks gave her face the impression of always being on the verge of a smile. Her eyes were light brown, almost translucent, as if he could look right through them and they could do the same to him. Her lips were soft and plump, and they smiled now as she looked toward him in the crowded elevator and nodded. Now that he was facing her, he could see that her curves were filled out in every direction—supple, full, inviting.

Rashad glanced at the floor number when the elevator bell rang, frustrated that he couldn't continue his perusal but mindful that it was probably for the best.

Their conversation erupted again—and as easily as it had before—as soon as they got to his car, which was in the parking garage right across the street from the Torpedo Factory.

"Can we park here?" Michelle asked. "I'll be driving again by next week. My car's only in the shop for a couple of days."

Rashad hid his disappointment and explained the terms of the lot.

"There were other lots listed," she said. "I'll check those, too."

"Before class started, you were saying that you aren't an artist as yet."

Michelle laughed. "I would love to say yes. But no. I love to draw and paint and want to learn how to really do it. I'm a student in the Department of Journalism in the School of Communication at Howard—"

"I went to Howard, as well, up through the MFA in design. Go Bisons!"

"Uh. Yeah. Go Bisons," Michelle echoed halfheartedly. Both of them laughed.

"I do support my home team," Michelle clarified.

"But you don't follow sports."

Michelle shook her head as they were getting into the car. "I'm an advertising student, and I want to be able to do original artwork for my advertising. We have to have a portfolio before we graduate, so now's the time to learn. What about you? Why are you in the class?"

"I finished a few years ago, and I work as a graphic designer for a web design firm in downtown D.C."

"Really?" Michelle said. "That sounds impressive. Congratulations."

Rashad took his eyes off the road for a couple seconds and glanced over to see if she was serious. She seemed sincere, and that felt good.

"It's not that impressive, but thank you. Anyway, I like being able to do my own thing rather than cutting and pasting all the time. I figure the more I know about drawing and the better I am at it, the more I can do and the better my work will be. My goal is to do more computer-based drawing, but you have to start with the fundamentals."

"They have all of that at the Corcoran College of Art and Design. I wanted to take Digital Design I, but their prices are incredible, even to audit."

The excitement in Michelle's voice seemed to light up the car with energy. Rashad liked that.

"I checked there, too," Rashad said. "It's only more expensive because they offer regular college courses at regular college prices. The Art League offers some range, as well. We'll have to see what's listed for next semester. Why aren't you taking this at Howard? It could be part of your regular tuition."

Michelle sighed heavily. "I wish I could. I might be able to take a class or two later on, but now I can't. I just started back at school, and they only took some of my credits. So to get out in the time I want, I have a full part-time load. I'll see as I go on."

"Hey, do you know where we are?"

"I have no idea."

Both of them laughed again.

"I might have to meet you before our next class so you can follow me in."

Michelle held her hand up. "No need. I have a zillion D.C. area street maps. I can't thank you enough for the ride home. Not everyone would have offered."

"It's no problem, really. I'm not that far from you, and it's my pleasure."

"Still, thank you."

Rashad heard the earnestness in Michelle's voice and acquiesced.

"You're welcome."

Then he had a thought. "If you ever need a ride again, or if you ever want to carpool and save on gas, let me know." It would be great to ride with her on a regular basis, get to know her better. He had to stop and remind himself that she was married.

"Okay, I will. But for now, I just want my car back. I'm lost without it, and I didn't want to miss our first class, so I'm learning even more about the Metro."

"And you already know that pretty well."

"Yes, I do."

"I take it you haven't been in D.C. long. Did you come for school? How long have you been here?"

"You know," she said, "you don't have to make small talk. I'd appreciate the ride home regardless."

"I want to know. You seem very nice, and it's good to know someone in our class—just in case I need to get a homework assignment or something."

That wasn't all that Rashad was thinking, but it was all that he could say without the risk of offending her. He couldn't let on that he was taken with her smile and her laughter and… What was he doing? The woman was married.

Out of the corner of his eye, he could see her peering at him, trying to determine whether he was actually interested or just chatting.

"Okay," she finally said. "I've been in the D.C. area for two years."

The laughter started low in Rashad's throat and bubbled up to the surface, getting louder along the way until it finally broke free.

She gave his shoulder a light swat, but she was laughing, as well.

"I'm sorry. Two years, and you only know the Metro?"

"Well, I didn't have a car the whole time. And I have work and—"

"You mean you haven't gotten out very much."

"Okay, no. I haven't."

Rashad wanted to say that he would make sure she got out more, but he didn't know how to say that without implying what he really meant—that he wanted to take her out. He shook his head, pondering it.

"Street maps, I told you. I have street maps."

Both chuckled again.

"And I do know where we are now."

"That's because we're in Greenbelt now—we're almost at your door."

"Well, yes."

She smiled, and he loved her smile.

"What's your address?"

When she said the number and street, Rashad realized that they really were almost at her door. He got a rather let-down feeling. *Strange.*

He drove through the maze of buildings in the apartment complex until he found hers; then he pulled up to the walk to let her out.

"Again," Michelle said, "I can't thank you enough. Really."

"*De nada.* I'll see you in class next week—homework in hand."

"Yes, you will. It was nice meeting you, and I'm glad to know someone else in the class. Let me grab my portfolio from the backseat so I can go get to my son."

"Sweet dreams."

He shouldn't have said that; he should have simply said goodbye. But somehow this woman made him think of just that—sweet dreams. Now he had to figure out why.

"Good night," she said.

On the way home, Rashad was aware of the quiet in the car, the absence of the energy that Michelle had brought to it. He pulled into his garage, turned off the engine and followed the walkway to his front door, still wondering what kind of spell had come over him.

He picked up his mail from behind the mail slot in the door and turned on the living room light. He looked around the room with new eyes and saw that he would be pleased to have her in it. His Ralph Lauren leather living room set had a high shine, and the Amish wood pieces matched it perfectly. Nothing in the room was frilly or feminine, but that was to be expected.

Unfortunately, nothing in the room was child-friendly, either. For the first time, he noticed the beveled edges of the glass coffee table, the sharp corners of the end tables and the points protruding from the wrought iron magazine rack. *Ouch.* There were also breakable things everywhere—the sculpture on one of the end tables, the glass he'd left on the coffee table that morning, the picture frames on the other end table.

But how old was Michelle's son? She barely seemed old enough to be married with a child, so he couldn't be that old.

Rashad whistled, and Shaka Zulu, his Yorkshire terrier, came bounding in from the kitchen.

"Hey, fella. Were you eating this late? Why didn't you come when I got home? You mad at me for being out so late?" He scratched the dog under the chin. "You're a child-friendly little one, aren't you? Okay, I'm talking to the dog now." What was it about that woman?

Actually, she seemed about his age, mid-twenties. Maybe early twenties. According to his brothers, that was more than old enough to be married with responsibilities, but Rashad put his brothers and their ribbing out of his mind.

Shaka followed him upstairs to his bedroom, where Rashad began changing from the long day. He loved that art class, but Wednesdays would be hell from here on—at least for eight more weeks. It also meant that he couldn't stay at work late on hump day anymore.

Actually, he'd be glad to start leaving work on time if he could show Michelle some of the city. And there she was again—on his mind.

Rashad had dated during and after college, but not seriously. He was used to meeting women, going out, having a good time. He wasn't used to liking a woman so much immediately, especially one who was off the market anyway.

And this one wasn't really his type. It stumped him. But maybe that meant they were destined to be friends. He could live with that—or so he thought. But as he climbed into bed, he thought of Michelle's ample curves and sighed.

Chapter 3

Michelle pulled her satchel from under her chair and starting dropping in her supplies.

"I'm glad to see that you made it here all right," Rashad said from the seat next to her.

"Yes, I did. Thank you very much. Hey," Michelle said to Rashad. They were both packing up after their second class at the Art League.

"Yep?"

"Is it okay if we exchange numbers? Only in case we ever have to miss a class or need a ride or something like that. I wouldn't pester you."

"You could never pester me," Rashad said. He wrote his numbers on Michelle's page of notes. "That one's my cell phone. This is my landline. Call me for anything. And this is my email. I check it all the time. Put yours here—if you're sure it's okay." He held out his notes.

"Yes, it's fine. I trust you not to go crazy with my number, but if I catch you putting it on a restroom wall, we'll fight."

He chuckled. "No, I wouldn't."

Rashad turned back to his portfolio and opened to a page. "Look at this. With all the design classes I've taken, I've never learned this trick."

Michelle looked at the abstract of an apple running.

"That's wonderful. You're already an artist."

"Not yet, love. Let's just say I'm working in my field. Let's see one of yours."

Michelle was hesitant but opened her portfolio to one of their assignments. It was a cubist form of a female nude against a brick wall.

"Wow. You're already an artist, too."

"Not yet, but I'm trying. I think this one will look good with color. I'm going to paint it over the weekend and see if I can link it to a women's organization or something. Maybe they'll want it, and that way I might be able to put it in my portfolio."

"I'm sure they will want it. It's beautiful, and I can already see it with color."

"I want to use various shades on the body—like a representation of multicultural women uniting or something like that. And— Never mind. I'm just yammering on."

"No, don't stop. I like it when you're excited about something," Rashad said. "I want to hear more, but everyone's leaving. Hey, do you have half an hour? We can stow supplies in my car and walk along the waterfront so that we can talk a little more. If not, I understand. Your son's waiting."

"No, I can stay for a while. Let me just check on the little one and update them that I'll be running late. I'll be back here in two minutes."

Michelle headed to the restroom to make her phone call and found that she was as excited about the prospect of walking along the waterfront with Rashad as she was about finishing her piece and, she hoped, getting it accepted somewhere.

"Hey, honey. It's Mommy….I know. I'll be on my way soon….You let Mrs. Miller put you to sleep now, and I'll carry you home when I get there. And brush your teeth well, young man….Let me talk to Mrs. Miller."

Mrs. Miller was fine keeping Andre for an extra half hour, so the night was set. Michelle found herself checking her hair in the mirror and applying more lipstick. Yes, she was excited about being out somewhere—and out with him. But that wouldn't do, would it? He hadn't actually shown any interest, at least not that kind of interest. She took a breath and went back to the classroom to collect her things.

"Do you know whether we have to turn in our portfolios at any point?" Rashad asked.

"Yes, we do. Three times. That's why we're supposed to number the assignments."

"You're right. I remember that now from last week. That didn't make it into my notes. How's the little one? Do you have time now, or do you need to get home?"

Rashad's voice dropped on the last question, as though he'd be disappointed if she had to leave. It was just a hint, but it made Michelle smile.

"I have time," she said, gathering her things. They started toward the elevators. "I bought an extra half hour, which is actually an extra hour, as I already gave myself half an hour of leeway—just in case."

"Excellent. My car is in the lot across the street again, and you can follow me to Greenbelt instead of using a street map, so you'll get home quickly."

Rashad chuckled after he said it, and so did Michelle, but she also rapped his arm with the back of her hand.

"No teasing the directionally challenged art student."

"I'm sorry. I couldn't resist. But I can lead you home."

"You don't have to, but it would be nice of you. My car's in this lot, too. I'm the used Ford Fiesta over there. I'll be right back."

While Rashad went over to his Kompressor, a Mercedes-Benz, Michelle headed to her Fiesta. It reminded her of the differences between them. Their ages were close, but he was finished with school and obviously doing well. She had gotten off track and was just starting over. He was where she wanted to be. No, he was where she *would* be one day—her and her son.

After storing their supplies, they recrossed the street and joined the groups sauntering along the Potomac. Michelle looked down at herself. She had on her usual bargain casual clothes—this time it was a green chiffon tank top with a green sweater, jeans and her usual flats. If she'd known they were going to hang out, she'd have dressed up a bit.

It was late September and a bit cool, so Rashad had put on his blazer when he'd dropped things off at his car. His tie was probably still in the car, but even without it, she could tell from the cut of his suit that he wore good quality to work. His black wing tip dress shoes gleamed. Again—the differences between them.

"What are you thinking?"

Rashad stirred her from thoughts she didn't want to express, but she didn't know what else to say.

She took a breath. "I was thinking that you've made it, and I haven't as yet—*as yet* being the operative words. I wanted to be finished with school by now, to be in my career. I guess I'm a little jealous."

"Don't be. You'll get there soon. And you have something to show for your time that I don't. A son, a family."

"That's true. And that's part of the reason I'm not finished as yet. But I'll get there. I have to."

It was just after ten and had gotten dark. The lights from the promenade were reflected on the water, and boats moored along the harbor bobbed slightly in the flow of the Potomac. There were fewer families out now and more couples. Michelle and Rashad walked close together in the quiet that had sprung up between them.

Rashad broke their silent interlude. "What were you saying before about the piece that you're going to paint this weekend?"

"I was thinking that I'd check with a few women's shelters and places like that—Women's Space, Agatha's House, that kind of thing."

"I think it would fit perfectly. It will be in your real portfolio sooner than you know."

"Thank you for the confidence."

"Don't forget I've seen it. Hey, I can help with the graphics if you need it."

"No." Michelle chuckled. "I wouldn't be able to add it to my portfolio then, could I?"

"I see your point. Do you know how to import photographs and stuff like that?"

"Enough to do a project, and I have some classmates to call when I need help with directions for things like that."

"Count me in, as well."

"Okay. Thank you."

They had passed several boats anchored along the waterfront and had now gotten to the Chart House, which was still open, at least for the next twenty minutes, so they decided to get a seat on the upper terrace overlooking the Potomac and have virgin daiquiris, as both were driving.

"How old is your son?"

The thought of her son made Michelle smile. "Andre is four. He's my whole heart."

"Aw. But four? You seem too young to have a four-year-old son."

"I've just gone back to school, but I'm twenty-five."

"I thought women weren't supposed to tell their ages and that men weren't supposed to ask."

"I know, but I never understood why. How old are you?"

"I'm twenty-seven," Rashad answered. "So this is your second time in school?"

"Yes, I started, but then came Andre, and there was just too much going on in my life."

"Andre's father?"

Michelle felt herself tense up, but she forced her shoulders to relax.

"I married right out of high school. Andre came a few years later."

"Wow. Right out of high school? I don't think I was mature enough to even think about marriage then."

"Well, I might not have been, either, but I did. I was a little wild in my younger days."

"Were you? I couldn't tell that from knowing you now."

"Hmm." Michelle thought briefly about her marriage and the toll it had taken on her. Maybe she had lost a bit of her spark, but she had spent the past two years trying to get some of it back. "I was. I partied. I went for the bad boy. I did whatever my parents said not to do. But I don't like to talk about the past. I want to focus on the future."

"And you guys have been in D.C. for two years?"

"Don't start with me now."

"I wasn't starting. I was just asking."

"Yes, we've been here for two years. I manage a coffeehouse downtown—Dupont Circle. I started out as a regular employee just after I came here. It's actually worked out. They let me do early morning and weekend hours, so that I can work full-time, go to school and be with my son in the evenings."

"So you're working your way through school and raising a son. That's a lot."

"I have good support. My cousin Nigel lives here, and his wife is a godsend."

"Where are you all from originally?"

"Charleston, South Carolina."

"Aha. I thought I caught a slight Southern drawl here and there."

Michelle swatted at Rashad playfully, but he caught her hand before it hit and held it for a moment—a long moment.

When he released her hand, Michelle had to shake her head to clear the questions in her mind and release the flutter from her stomach.

"We Charlestonians are proud of our Southern heritage. I do still have the accent, but I can turn it on and off now that I've been in D.C. for so long. You should hear me when I go home." Michelle then checked her watch. "Actually, we need to finish our drinks. They'll be closing soon."

"Oh, you're right," Rashad said, glancing around. "I think they've closed the doors already. They're just waiting for us stragglers. Hey, if you can stay a little late next week, we should walk along King Street. They stay open later, and they have bunches of shops and galleries—art, jewelry—"

"I know. My cousin's wife—her name is Regina—she co-owns a mosaic and beadwork studio and gallery not far up King Street." Michelle stood as Rashad paid their tab. "That's how I first found out about the Torpedo Factory. What about you? Are you from D.C. originally?"

"No, but my family is from Baltimore, and we'd come down every so often." Rashad also rose, and they headed back to the promenade. "Then I came to D.C. to go to Howard, and then I stayed here to work. I've been here awhile. I don't know where everything is, but I know most stuff."

"Between work and home, I don't get out a lot."

"Now I know why you haven't seen much of the D.C.

area. I'd like to show some of it to you if you'll let me." His tone was soft, but then he straightened, and in a matter-of-fact voice, he added, "If that's all right."

"Maybe after the semester is over. I can do more over the winter break and over the summer."

They were retracing their steps along the waterfront, taking their time back to their cars.

"Tell me about being a graphic designer. What attracted you to that?"

"I love art, and I love working on the computer."

"Ugh. That's where we differ. I like paper and pencil or paint. I don't know what I'll do when we can't read books, actual books, anymore."

"I like that, too, but I like the computer, as well. And mind you, the day is not far off when everything you read will be on a computer tablet of some kind."

"No, no. I don't want to hear it." Michelle covered her ears with her hands. "La, la, la—" She interrupted herself laughing, and Rashad started laughing, as well.

"Okay. I'm past my rage against the future. You may go on."

"I'm not sure I should. I work for a web design firm, so everything we do is for the computer. But there are graphic designers in a variety of fields. I took to web design because I had to learn how to do one for a project, and I got hooked. It's great bringing an organization to life on the screen. I guess I like what I do."

"You're very lucky."

"And you?" Rashad asked. "Why advertising?"

"I love the artistic side of it," Michelle said. "I don't know much about the business side of it as yet. I don't like the idea of fooling people or luring people with false promises. I want to produce art, and advertising is what I want to do because it's art that everybody sees. It's art without the hundred-dollar ticket price for the orchestra seat."

"So you're a Marxist revolutionary about art—art for the masses!"

"In a way. And don't knock Marxism. From what I've read, Marx was quite brilliant. That's my way of saying he's dense as hell."

Both laughed.

"He was damn near incomprehensible sometimes," Rashad agreed. "I've dabbled, as well."

"Kudos to us for trying," Michelle said. "High five."

Michelle raised her hand, and Rashad met it.

"Are you sure you're not a sports fan?"

"Absolutely sure."

They were at Michelle's car now and had paused. Rashad seemed as reluctant as she was about the end of the evening. It had felt like being on vacation to Michelle. Adult conversation with a handsome man, an hour in which she didn't have to be anywhere, talking with someone who seemed to be genuinely interested in what she was saying, what she was thinking. It was like paradise.

Michelle unlocked her door, and Rashad leaned toward her and reached around her to open the door. But they still stood there.

Rashad leaned toward her in the dim light of the garage, and, for a moment, Michelle thought that he was going to kiss her. She held her breath and felt her heart begin to pound in her chest.

But just as quickly as it happened, the moment was over. Rashad straightened, and Michelle wondered if she had misread his body movements. She felt her face flush with embarrassment, wondering if he could tell that she'd thought he was about to—

"Follow behind me. I won't run any yellow lights or anything like that. But honk if you start to fall behind."

Rashad had turned and had taken several steps toward his car, but he turned back.

"How long have you been married?"

"Married?"

"Your husband is a lucky man. And you were married right out of high school, so that's about…six years?"

"I'm not married anymore."

"Huh? I thought…"

Michelle saw the confusion in Rashad's crinkled brow.

"I was divorced a little while before I moved to D.C. That was one of the reasons I moved—to leave that past behind, so to speak."

"But before I asked how long you guys had been here."

"I thought you meant me and my son. We've been here two years. I didn't know that you thought—"

"Wow. I guess I just assumed that you were married—still married."

"I guess I wasn't clear."

There was a pause in which each seemed to be recalculating—tracing their conversations to detect the flaw that had led to the misunderstanding and reassessing what had just happened in light of the clarification.

Still, Michelle wasn't sure what to think, and it was she who broke the silence.

"I had better get going. I have to get my son from the sitter."

Her words seemed to awaken Rashad from a reverie, and he refocused his eyes on her. He stared at her a moment before he spoke. "Okay. Yes. Just follow behind me."

He took a couple of steps toward his car and then turned back again.

"Next Wednesday let's have dinner in Old Town Alexandria after class and window-shop along King Street—if you can get home late again."

"Okay," Michelle answered. "I'll check and email you if the sitter doesn't mind."

"Don't forget."

"I won't."

Michelle followed Rashad as far as Beltway Plaza on Greenbelt Road, wondering all the while what had just happened.

When he turned off Beltway Road to the street leading to her apartment complex, Rashad stopped and waved her past him.

There was no traffic, so she pulled up alongside him.

"Can you get home from here?" he teased.

"Don't you play with me when I can't reach you to strangle you. The real question," she said, "is whether or not I can find my way from class again."

"Can you?"

"No."

They cracked up.

Michelle waved, passed him and continued on as he made a U-turn and headed back to Beltway Road.

She picked up a sleeping little Andre from two doors down and carried him home to put him in his own bed. Once that was done, she started to change. She had to get to bed right away because she had to be at the coffeehouse early the next morning. She would get Andre ready and drop him off with Mrs. Miller, who would walk him to school.

She cherished Mrs. Miller. It mattered more than anything having people around whom she could trust, especially with her child. She paid Mrs. Miller, of course, but what Mrs. Miller did for her couldn't be counted in money. She took Mrs. Miller grocery shopping and had her over for Sunday supper sometimes and did whatever else she could, but it didn't seem like enough. Mrs. Miller and her cousin Nigel and his wife, Regina, and her boss at the coffeehouse allowed her to do the things she hoped would get her life back on track after that fiasco of a marriage.

She had even spent a night out after her art class with

almost no notice. And that was what was really on Michelle's mind, keeping her awake.

She kept replaying the moment when it had seemed that Rashad wanted to kiss her, and she kept wondering about his reaction when she'd told him that she wasn't married. It was clearly news to him, but he hadn't come back to kiss her. Perhaps he didn't want her if she was actually within reach. Or maybe he hadn't been about to kiss her and was just being polite to let her get over her embarrassment. But then he had asked her out the next week, or was that only to continue their friendship from class?

Deep down, she wanted him to be interested, and that's what scared her.

It was funny to think that after being divorced for two and a half years, the prospect of a date would perplex her, but it did. Was next week a date?

Michelle fell asleep wondering what the following Wednesday would bring but determined to let it be whatever it turned out to be. In her mind, life was looking up. She could at least imagine having a date, and she was finally getting her life in order after the merry-go-round marriage she'd had.

Don't forget to check with Mrs. Miller and email Rashad. That was her last coherent thought before she nodded off, and her dreams were tinged with possibility.

Chapter 4

Rashad sank into the leather sectional that lined the back of his brother Marcus's law office. Rashad was the youngest of four brothers, and all were now gathered in Marcus's office because they had planned—before Rashad knew about his class dates—to go to a Washington Redskins game. He had called to bow out, but he came to see his brothers off. Now all of the brothers—Derrick, Marcus, Keith, and Rashad himself—had arrived.

"I'm just explaining," Rashad said. "Why I can't go tonight. I have a class, and I'm having dinner with a classmate afterwards."

"Is this dinner with a man or a woman?" Derrick, the oldest brother, asked.

Rashad rolled his eyes.

"It's a woman," Keith said. He was sitting next to Rashad and nudged Rashad's shoulder.

"What does that prove—whether it's a man or woman?" Marcus said.

"Just because you're gay doesn't make the rest of us gay," Keith said. "We love you, bro. But this is a different story."

"If it was just dinner," Rashad explained, "I would reschedule, but I can't change the date and time of my class."

"Forget the class," Keith said. "We want to know about the date."

"Are you still playing," Derrick asked, "or are you getting serious?"

Rashad was the only one of his brothers not married, including Marcus, the gay one, and it was never long before they started their ribbing and tried to get him to find the right one and "settle down." Rashad let his head fall back and then shook it, looking at the ceiling. It was starting.

"Rashad hasn't been serious about anyone his whole life," Derrick said.

"Hey, I've always been up front about not wanting to get serious."

"That's to your credit," Marcus said. "But what about getting serious for a change?"

"I'll know when it's time to get serious," Rashad answered. "I'll know when I find the right one."

"I don't know," Keith said, already trying to control his laughter. "I've seen you out with a couple of, how shall I say, not-so-comely women."

This exaggeration was designed to get Rashad's gall up. They all knew that he dated lookers.

"Okay. Let me alone." He panned his index fingers, pointing at all his brothers. "I can whip all of your behinds individually. Remember that."

Rashad was the youngest but also by far the tallest of the four at six feet and two inches. And his brothers' ribbing did get his gall up. He had dated only casually partly because he had in mind a model prototype of the woman he would marry, and he had not met her yet, so he had never really been serious. Actually, he resented the pressure his brothers put on him to conform, but he found that it subsided more quickly if he ignored them and didn't let on that they were getting on his last nerve.

"It's not that it isn't fun to play," Derrick said. "But there comes a time to settle down."

Those were the words he hated. Rashad raised his palms in desperation, then let them slam down on his thighs.

"Here we go again."

"Just trying to school you the right way, baby brother," Marcus said, backing up Derrick.

"What we mean—"

Rashad cut off Keith. He was the last one married and the least serious of the bunch about everything except his marriage.

"No, we're not going there today. And you, brother of mine, are the last one who should be talking about being serious."

His other brothers cracked up, which was not quite what Rashad had intended.

"We're not on me today," Keith said, almost pouting. He added, "Thank heavens."

Rashad stood as Trevor, Marcus's partner, opened the door and came inside.

"I have to get on it," Rashad said. "I have to make it to Old Town Alexandria from here in rush hour traffic. Hey, Trevor." He greeted the other man with a brief hug. "You taking my place tonight?"

"Apparently so."

Marcus got up from behind his desk and came over to them, first hugging his partner hello then clapping Rashad on the back and pulling him in for a similar hug goodbye. Derrick got up from his chair and Keith from the sectional, and both also came over to hug Rashad.

"I'm sorry I can't make it tonight, you guys. We don't get together enough."

"Hey," Derrick said, "Thanksgiving is next month, and I think the next game is before that."

Rashad and Keith did their thing, a brief hug and then a smacking of closed fists.

"I'll see you all then," Rashad said. "If not before."

He left his brother's firm and made it to his meter before it expired.

His brothers had riled him, but they also had him thinking. Tonight was actually something of a date (though he would never say that to his brothers), and he didn't know if he needed to say something to Michelle about not getting too serious. It was generally the first thing out of his mouth—just so they couldn't point fingers later—but it hadn't even occurred to him to say anything to Michelle. But then he'd thought she was married. Now that he knew she wasn't, he still didn't want to say anything. He didn't want to chance chasing her away.

Something about her just set him at ease with himself. Yet she wasn't what he thought his ideal would be. He imagined a sleek, sexy, manicured professional type—a corporate lawyer in a tight-fitting skirt done up to the nines, assertive and in control but his (and only his) playmate. He'd had that fantasy since he was a teenager, hence the model types that he'd dated. But none of them had shared his interests or even his thoughts.

Michelle, on the other hand, sparked something inside him. He thought about her, waited for her email saying that she could stay late after class—which had finally come two days ago. It was the way her energy filled his car on the ride home, or the way he fantasized about her curves. She was beautiful, but not in a sleek, manufactured way. There was some fire to her, but there was also a sweetness about her, an unassuming quality.

He reached the Torpedo Factory Art Center without coming to any resolution and smiled when he saw her beat-up Ford Fiesta in the lot as he pulled in. Yes, there was something about this woman.

He didn't know quite what it was or what to do about it, and he didn't have time to figure it out right then, so he would let come what might.

He found her already there when he entered the classroom, and took his usual seat next to her.

"Did you still need a map to get here?"

"Don't start with me," she said, but then she chuckled and nodded her head. "Did you finish your homework?"

"Of course. And here I am with it, even though I'm missing a Redskins game with my brothers."

"Redskins?"

Rashad couldn't suppress his laughter, and other students in the class turned to look. He wanted to let them in on it, but he couldn't stop the laughter, so he just waved them away. When he could catch his breath, he turned back to Michelle.

"You don't know who the Redskins are?"

"I told you I don't follow sports. But has anybody thought about this name?"

Rashad chuckled more, but he could control the volume this time.

"I'm glad I amuse you," Michelle said. Then she put her hand on her hip and moved her head back and forth, getting real. "But this laughter at my expense has got to end."

"I'm sorry. I am. And, yes, I'm sure that the name has been a subject of debate."

Rashad was laughing again before he finished. After a firm look in his direction, Michelle joined in.

"Are we still on for tonight, or do you need to leave early to catch what you can of the game on television or something?"

"No, my brother-in-law got my ticket, and the game will show in reruns, so we're on. I guess that's the upside of missing the game. I don't have to miss tonight with you."

Michelle looked at him closely, perhaps judging his sincerity, but she didn't reply. She shrugged her shoulders and mouthed the word *okay.*

That was enough—that and the way she looked tonight. Though she was sitting down, he could see that she didn't have on her usual leggings or jeans. She had dressed a bit for tonight. Over what looked like a brown satin camisole, she had on a brown lace cover-up that fit close to her body and that went down to her thighs. She also had on brown palazzo pants that widened at the ankle, flaring out like a dress, and she had on low black heels. Instead of her usual sweater, a long, brown African mudcloth wrap hung on the back of her chair with her purse.

Her long hair had fresh curls at the ends, and a piece of material that matched her cover-up circled her head from her nape to her crown, ending in a neat knot above her left ear. If he was right, her face had a little extra makeup, as well, just enough so that he could see the extra care she'd taken.

It was enough to make Rashad look twice and value what he saw—a beautiful woman. He looked down at his standard white shirt and slacks and wished he'd done something else. At least he could grab his coat and tie from the car when they dropped off their portfolios.

"You look great tonight," he whispered as the teacher walked in.

She smiled and turned to the front of the class, which was all on composition and started with a slide show. For their first drawing exercise, they had to create an arrangement with twenty abstract and unrelated objects. This focused his attention on the task at hand, even if part of his mind was waiting for it to be over.

At the end of the class, they turned in the assignments from their portfolios, and he finally got a look at Michelle standing. In low heels, she was only a couple of inches shorter than he was.

"You must be something like five-eleven, right?"

"What?"

"Five feet eleven inches tall."

Her brow wrinkled, but she confirmed it. "Yes, how did you know?"

"I have about three inches on you, but not when you have on heels. You look great tonight."

"You said that before."

"I mean it again."

"Thank you."

Michelle had gathered up her things and turned to him. "Where to now?"

"What do you feel like eating?"

She made a guttural sound and slumped. "I hate that question. Anything. I feel like eating anything."

"I checked, and there's a little bit of just about everything around King Street."

Michelle held up her hand and waved for him to follow her. "Let's walk and talk before it gets too late."

"There's a burger place off King Street. Oh, there's a Southern place called King Street Blues. I think we can walk there from here. How about that?"

"Yes. There. Quick. Decisive. No pondering." Michelle chuckled. "I hate that question, but thank you for asking rather than just deciding. And, yes, Southern will be fine, but not fried. I can't gain another pound or my clothes won't fit, and I don't have wardrobe bucks until I pick up some extra hours at the coffeehouse over the summer."

Rashad knew Michelle well enough to let that go. But he filed the reference under possible things to get her for Christmas.

After they stored their portfolios and supplies, they decided to head straight for the restaurant rather than linger along King Street and chance having it close on them. Michelle had on her mudcloth wrap and looked like an African queen. Rashad took her hand as they maneuvered through the groups touring the street. She was leading, and he didn't want to lose her, but it felt good to have her hand for other reasons, too. She looked back at him and smiled, plunging them along through the crowd.

"Does this place ever quiet down?" he asked once they made it to the restaurant.

"I've been at Regina's shop until midnight, and there were still people in the streets," Michelle said.

"That's right. I'd almost forgotten. Did we pass it?"

"Yes, but I can point it out on the way back, when we have more time."

The restaurant was still open, and they were seated right away.

Rashad took Michelle's hands in his while they waited for their late-night meal. He saw her get still and quiet, but she didn't take her hands away. Instead, she smiled at him.

"I like the feel of your hands," she said. "They're strong."

"Yours are soft. I like that, too."

Unfortunately, it wasn't long before their dinner arrived, and Rashad had to let Michelle's hands go for what they'd ordered. The ribs were tender, the cornbread was moist, the greens were well peppered and the cobbler was juicy. It was a real Southern meal.

"Does it compare to what you get down home?" he asked.

"Yes, it does, but no one can top my uncle's ribs or my mother's cornbread and cobbler. This is like home when you're on vacation."

"Good. I'm glad you like it."

"What about your family traditions? How many brothers and sisters do you have?"

"I have three brothers, no sisters."

"But you said your brother-in-law got your Redskins ticket."

"One of my brothers is gay. His partner is my brother-in-law."

"Good for them."

"I'm glad you're cool with that. Thank you."

"No thanks needed. Was your family okay when he came out?"

"Long story short—no." Rashad chuckled. "At least not my father. But he got over it, I think. I hope so for my brother. What about you? Any siblings?"

"Nope, just me."

"Michelle the bad girl."

"Well, I did grow up."

Rashad could tell there was more to that, but seeing that Michelle didn't go on, he let it go. They talked about art for the rest of their meal. When they turned to the cobbler, the conversation changed. With the main course gone, he regained her hand, and when he caressed her fingers, hers caressed his back.

"I know it's soon, but I really, really like you," Rashad heard himself say. "I—I don't know what else I planned to say. Just that, I guess."

"I like you a great deal, too."

"Do you date much—since your divorce, I mean?"

Michelle got quiet and still again; even the fingers that had been caressing his ceased to move.

"No, I haven't dated at all. I've just been trying to recreate my life—to arrange things so that I could go back to school, work, raise my son. It doesn't leave time for a whole lot, and I haven't really been interested in more than that for a while."

"Would you be interested in dating now?"

She shrugged. "It's hard to balance everything. I'm not sure if there are enough hours in a day—or a week."

She hadn't gotten his real question.

"What about me? Could you see yourself dating me?"

"I think so," she answered.

Rashad's chest swelled, but he tried not to show it.

"What about you?" Michelle asked. "What have your relationships been like?"

Now it was Rashad's turn to get quiet; he had to admit what he didn't want to admit to this particular woman.

"I've dated a lot but nothing serious. I've been waiting for the right person."

Michelle squinted her eyes and did a double take. "Nothing serious? What does that mean?"

"My relationships," Rashad said, "have all been mutually superficial. I hate to say that, but it's true."

Michelle took a deep breath and looked Rashad straight in the eyes with those translucent brown pools of hers. When she finally spoke, it was slow, and he could read the disappointment in her tone.

"My life is a bit too complicated right now to have a mutually superficial relationship, Rashad. I can't do that."

They had finished their dessert, and she started to get up.

She turned back, looking around the restaurant. "We need the check."

"I'll get that, but wait."

She had started to leave again.

"Wait. Don't go. I'm not asking you to do that. I don't want that with you." This much, at least, was true. Now that he knew she wasn't married, he was even more interested in her. He could allow himself to be interested in her.

"What do you want with me, Rashad?"

That he didn't know.

"I don't know. I only know that I almost kissed a married woman when I thought you were married, and I haven't been able to stop thinking about you since I met you, and I've never talked to anyone the way I can talk to you. That's all I know. What do you want with me?"

He had gotten hold of her hand, and he drew her back to the table.

"I don't know," she finally said. "I guess I just know that I like spending time with you."

Rashad couldn't help but smile.

"But I don't want a casual thing."

"Deal. Let's see where this can go, and no casual thing. Either we become friends and nothing else, or we become something real. No in-between."

"Deal."

They both took deep breaths as the rough patch between them fell away. Now they could relax.

He paid the tab, and, as they left the restaurant, he put his hand on the small of her back. She looked up at him and smiled.

"I like it when you touch me that way."

"I want to touch you more," Rashad said softly.

"Let's not rush into things," Michelle responded. "Let's figure out what we want first."

Still, he saw a shudder move through her shoulders and could tell that she was responding to his touch, his voice.

"Okay."

They walked slowly back toward North Union Street, window-shopping along the way and stepping inside some of the stores that were still open. They paused in front of the art galleries and a couple of advertisements to talk about the pieces using their newly acquired knowledge from class.

Rashad had taken Michelle's hand, and she took his arm as they strolled. She pointed out the mosaic and beadwork studio that belonged to her cousin's wife, and Rashad wanted to go in—mainly to meet some of her family but also because the pieces were fabulous. Unfortunately, it was late enough that the studio was closed. They would have to come back another day.

This time, when they got to Michelle's Ford Fiesta, Rashad took her in his arms and pressed her body against his. He expected her to hesitate after their conversation, but she lifted her arms to his neck, smiling, and tipped upward on her toes to meet his lips.

The soft pressure of her lips and the floral aroma of her perfume filled his senses, and the way her curves pressed against him made his body rigid. When they broke from the most sensual kiss he had ever had, Rashad teetered back, drunk on the moment.

"Was that as good as kissing a married woman?" Michelle asked.

"That was infinitely better," he said and let out a long, shaky breath, his body wanting more.

Michelle gasped and looked at her watch.

"Oh, no. I'm going to be late getting my son."

"How long do you have?"

"Fifteen minutes."

"Let's go. You'll be late five minutes, at most. Honk if I get too far ahead of you."

Rashad turned toward his car, turned back to give Michelle one more brief kiss and they were off.

Chapter 5

Michelle stuck her hand inside the vase she had finished painting and handed it to Regina to go in the kiln.

"The flowers are done on this one."

"They're beautiful. Are you sure you don't want to be an artist?"

"I'm sure I do want to be an artist, and I want to apply it to advertising."

"I stand corrected. You'll do wonderfully."

"Thank you for the support. I need it."

"No, you don't. You're doing great."

Michelle painted in her spare time and sometimes did ceramics with her cousin Nigel's wife, Regina. It even brought in a bit of change for her now and then. But she did it because she loved it and because it was great to practice on something real, something that would be used.

She had this Saturday off from the coffeehouse, so she spent the morning doing homework and the rest of the day at Regina's, where Andre got to paint a piece of his own.

He would be staying the night with Nigel and Regina because Michelle had a date—a real Saturday date—with Rashad. She had only been about five minutes late the Wednesday before last, when she had stayed after class to have dinner, but she didn't want to risk being late after class anymore, and a Saturday gave them real time to spend together. Still, she hesitated.

"Are you sure you'll be okay with Andre tonight? You have little Sharon, as well, and she's only twelve months."

"Yes, Michelle. We've had him overnight before. He'll be fine with us. Go out for a change."

"I don't know."

"It's been over two years since your divorce, and you haven't seen anyone. Don't go from a wildflower to a weed. It's okay to have a life." Regina got close to her, ignoring her hesitation. "Is he cute?"

Michelle couldn't stop the smile that spread across her face. Regina gasped.

"He is! Tell me."

"Well, actually, he's a bit like Nigel. Not in looks, but in character. He's always doing something nice, and he's sweet and he's talkative."

And he has no idea what a wild girl I used to be or how horrible my marriage was. Michelle thought those things, but she didn't say them. It would have been admitting her flaws, and she didn't want to say them out loud, not even to her supportive cousin-in-law. *Oh, and he's only dated casually. But we have that cleared up, I think.*

"And he's as handsome as all get-out. It should be illegal to look as good as he does."

"Uh-huh. Sing it, sister. That never hurt," Regina said and chuckled.

"Oh, I don't know."

"Yes, you do. You go on and have a good time. It's been a while, so take it slowly, but it's time to get out there again.

Don't wait until college is over and then until your career is off the ground and then until Andre is grown and then until whatever it is. It will never be finished until you're finished. Nigel and I can watch Andre more, especially now that Sharon is here. And you watch Sharon for us more than enough. Let us do a little for you, too."

"You both do…so much for me. I don't know how to thank you."

"You just did, and you always do. Now go on. Get made up and hit the town."

"It's just dinner and a movie."

But Michelle smiled nevertheless. She was excited to go out with Rashad—for real.

"Where are you going?"

"I don't know. He says I haven't seen D.C. in the two years I've been here, and he wants me to see some of it. But we're starting with the basics."

Michelle had washed her hands and was gathering up her purse.

"I'm going to pop upstairs and see Andre before I go."

"Sure," Regina said, shooing her toward the door. "But don't take long."

"I won't."

After checking on Andre, Michelle hopped in her car and went home to get ready for the evening. She didn't have anything fancy, but it was only a movie, so something nice would do.

She was ready when Rashad buzzed her doorbell at six.

"Come in. The downstairs door is open, and I'm upstairs on the right."

In moments he appeared at her open door.

"Is that safe—for the downstairs door to be unlocked?"

"I don't know, but it always has been."

"You should mention that to whoever manages the building."

"Actually, I have. No change."

"We'll have to see about that."

Rashad had on a brightly colored shirt for a change, and he wore it with black slacks. He also had a heavy lamb's wool cardigan over one arm and a bag in the other hand.

"Is it cold out?"

"Not yet, but it will be tonight and at the movie. I should have left this in the car, but I took it off on the way up."

Michelle grabbed her sweater and purse, but Rashad was still looking around. "Where's Andre? I thought I would meet him. I brought him these."

He handed Michelle a bag of toys.

"He's at my cousin's. You didn't buy these, did you? Toys are expensive, and he has toys. You can't buy his approval, you know."

"I know, but I thought I'd try." Rashad chuckled. "Actually, most of these are my nephew's. He's too old for them now, so I thought I would pass them along. These are new."

Rashad pointed to games and learning programs that went with a computerized tablet.

"Trying to get him hooked on the computer early, I see. We do have one."

"I know. Or I figured—you being a student. But these are his very own, and all the new programs are for his age-group."

"Rashad, you didn't have to. This is too much."

"No, like I said, my nephew outgrew most of this. Here, this is for you."

He pulled a DVD from the bottom of the bag.

"I didn't know about flowers or chocolate."

Michelle took a serious step back. "Don't tell me you didn't know about chocolate," she said, her eyes sparkling with humor.

"Well, I guess I know now. But what kind? See. Too many options."

"Anything with nuts—peanuts, almonds, pecans."

Rashad laughed at the passion in her voice. Then she stepped back to him and took the DVD he was holding out. It was *The Color Purple.*

"Aw. I love this movie. And I don't have it."

"I'm glad. I thought you might like it. You think in color. Look at your place."

Michelle followed Rashad's gaze to her living room. The furniture was worn but colorful, and her walls were full of art, what she could afford, which was her own and her son's. It did make for a rather gaudy presentation. She laughed at the thought.

"What?" Rashad asked.

"It's actually quite gaudy. I hadn't noticed before."

"It's not gaudy. It's bright. And it fills in for what you don't have or can't afford right now."

"That it does. Thank you, Rashad, for the movie and the toys for Andre. You didn't have to, really."

Michelle didn't know how to truly express her thanks. It was all more than she could have imagined and just like Rashad, as she was coming to see.

"I wanted to. Don't give it another thought. Are you ready to go?"

"Yes. Where are we off to?"

"Have you been to Gallery Place, Chinatown, in northwest D.C.?"

"I've driven through it a couple of times."

"Good. I thought we could go to Clyde's for an early dinner—they have just about everything. And the movie theater there has fourteen cinemas, so there should be something that we like. Does that sound okay?"

"It sounds great. Oh, can we find parking down there, or should we take the train in?"

"Parking is a block over. If your shoes are comfortable, we'll be fine."

"They are," Michelle said. "Let's go." Then she paused. "Wait. Who's driving?"

"I figure I am—only because I know where we're going."

"Okay. As long as you're not still poking fun."

Rashad pursed his lips in the cutest little pout. "Would I do that?"

Michelle flicked her finger against his arm. "Yes," she said. "You would." But she was still taken by his childlike pucker and smiled.

Clyde's was packed, and when she got to see the atmosphere, she understood why. It was lively, but it was quiet enough to talk, and they did have just about everything.

Michelle rolled her shoulders and stretched her head to either side after they sat down.

"I'm so glad I didn't have to work today. I got so much done."

"Tired?"

"No, I just needed a stretch."

"How do you manage on what you make at the coffeehouse, even as a manager? Is that too personal to ask? You don't have to answer."

"No, that's fine. I would wonder if I wasn't me. I get some child support and alimony from my ex-husband, and between that and work, I can pay for things around the house. For school I take out student loans, and my cousin Nigel helps a little with that. He's…wonderful, and he's like you—giving. I can only imagine what I'll need to pay him back."

Rashad took her hand, and Michelle felt a tingle move up her spine.

"He wants you to pay him back?"

"No, but I will. I wouldn't feel right if I didn't. He tells me that we're family, and that if anything, I should 'pay it forward,' like the movie, where you help someone else. But I will pay him back."

"I can tell you will. What are your plans for your career?"

"I don't know in detail. Right now I'm just working on finishing my degree and making myself as marketable as possible. That's why I want a good portfolio for school. I'm hoping that I can get a good entry-level job and keep moving upward."

"Do you save for Andre's education?"

"Actually, I do, out of child support. I couldn't before, but I do now. It means sticking to a tight budget, but I'm used to that."

Michelle saw the question in Rashad's eyes, but she didn't want to say more about the past and was glad that he let it go.

"Are there plans for your career?" she asked.

Rashad started caressing her fingers, and Michelle felt herself shudder. It was so sensual, like it had been on their other dinner date. Michelle couldn't keep from caressing back. She couldn't stop the heat from rising in the pit of her stomach.

"I make a decent living now, but I think I'll want more when I have a family, and I want to do more artistic work. Right now my goal is to keep doing good work and expanding my credentials so that I can get those pay increases and maybe open my own design firm one day."

"That's a good plan once you've gotten as far as you have."

Michelle felt another twinge of jealousy, but she let it go. She would be okay one day. She didn't expect Rashad's next line of inquiry.

"What's it like raising a son? What is Andre like?"

"Andre is a sweet pea, as much as he's been through."

She'd said too much again, dang it. She had to stop

opening the door to things she wanted to forget. She hoped that Rashad had missed it or would let it pass, but he didn't.

"What has he been through, Michelle?"

She wanted to say something that would close the door on that question, but she didn't know what.

"He… My marriage was difficult, and it ended badly. That's not the example I wanted to set for my child, but he's just a sweet kid—in spite of all that."

Rashad nodded and let the question pass, and Michelle was grateful.

"But raising a child is wonderful. It's so much responsibility. His whole life right now is up to me. I don't know how to explain it."

"I think I know what you mean."

"And the love of a child is totally unconditional. It's…a blessing. I guess I'm not really religious, but I don't know any other word."

To show his understanding, Rashad rubbed her hand. When he was finished, Michelle went back to caressing his fingers. She liked that better. She saw the look in his eyes when she did it, and he seemed to like it better, as well.

Their dinner arrived, and Michelle shook her head to get out of her thoughts. She and Rashad let go of each other's hands and pulled them from the table to get ready to eat. She had ordered catfish, and Rashad had gotten steak.

"One day we have to come back here for their burgers," he said. "I've heard they're great, but there's so much to choose from that all the times I've been here, I've gotten something else."

"Have you been here often?"

"Sometimes my brothers and I come here before or after a game or if we get together on a weekend."

"You and your brothers sound close."

"I guess we are, as much as they rib me."

"I wish I had a sister. Or a brother. Any sibling. I guess my cousin and his wife are as close as I come to that."

"Then I'm glad you have them. I want to meet them sometime."

"I hope you will. They're great people. Without Nigel, I wouldn't be in D.C. He was here first and helped me make the move. He drove me home to get more of my things. He helped me out financially until I had an income. He helped me get used to a more northern, more urban landscape. He encouraged me to go to Howard. He continues to help me with paying for it. He's been a godsend."

"One day," Rashad said, "I hope you'll feel close enough to me to let me help you."

"One day, I hope I won't need you—or anyone else—to help me."

"That day is coming."

"I know," Michelle said. "And I guess I know all that I've actually done on my own, as well."

"Exactly. You made the move. You're taking the classes and working and raising a son. You're my hero."

Michelle was touched by Rashad's words.

"I just have to remember to celebrate all that while I strive for more."

"Amen."

They ate quietly for a while, and the peace between them wasn't interrupted until their waiter came to offer them dessert.

"Let's split something," Michelle suggested.

"What? I could go for apple pie."

"I don't think so. Not when there's something called Chocolate Blackout Cake on the menu."

"I should have known about the chocolate," Rashad said, shaking his head.

Michelle laughed. "Yes indeed." She turned to the waiter. "We'll split the chocolate cake and ice cream."

"Yes, ma'am."

Michelle ate most of the cake, and Rashad had most of the ice cream. After that, they headed to the movie theater, selected the new version of *Les Misérables* and found a relatively unoccupied row in the back of the theater to watch it.

Rashad had brought his sweater, and Michelle was already wearing hers, but it was still chilly. Not long after the film started, she slipped her hands into Rashad's open cardigan to warm them. His chest heaved under her touch, and he glanced toward her.

"Sorry," she said. "I just wanted to warm my hands."

"No need for apologies. I don't mind if you do that again."

Michelle felt mischievous and raked her fingers along Rashad's chest. It heaved again, and he shifted in his seat.

"Okay, maybe I shouldn't have said you could do that again."

Michelle smiled and let her hands come to a rest. Rashad wrapped his arm around her, drawing her close to his warmth. She could feel the heat from his body as she rested her head on his shoulder, and his arm was like a blanket around her.

Without thinking about it, she ran her fingers over his chest again. Rashad turned toward her with a passionate look on his face that made her catch her breath, and before Michelle could react, he had drawn his hand inside her sweater and over her chest.

His touch filled her with desire, and her nipples tightened under his fingers. And he didn't stop. He caressed the taut peaks that his fingers had just made until she was shivering with each flicker, until a low murmur escaped her throat.

They teased each other like that on and off throughout the film, stopping when one had had too much or to hear a touching or rousing song. But one or the other would start up again after the interlude. Occasionally, Rashad dipped his head to kiss her forehead or her ear. It made Michelle shiver, but he couldn't really know what it did to her, the way it set her moisture flowing.

They sat up as the credits rolled and looked at one another. Her face felt flushed, and she was sure that the passion he saw there matched the passion in his own eyes.

"I have to get you home to Andre, don't I?" Rashad said.

"No, he's staying with Nigel and Regina and their little girl tonight."

Rashad looked into her eyes and spoke in a soft, deep voice that sent quivers into the pit of Michelle's stomach. "Come home with me," he said. "Let me make love to you."

Michelle had wanted to hear Rashad say something like that, but now that he had, she found herself reluctant to respond. Were they moving too fast? Was she ready for this? Would this be real, or would this be "mutually superficial"? Or were they meant to be just friends? She didn't know the answers to those questions, only that she wanted him as much as he wanted her and that she hadn't dated a sweeter man in all her life.

"We don't have to," he said. "We—"

"I want to, Rashad."

At the car Michelle had a thought. "Do you have...protection for us, or do we need to stop somewhere?"

"We're covered for that at my place."

"Okay."

Michelle opened the door and paused.

"Do you want me to drive?" she asked, breaking the tension between them.

"Can you find your way to your place from here?"

Michelle pursed her lips. "No."

"Well, then, you definitely can't find your way to mine."

They laughed, and Michelle wagged her finger at him. "You underestimate my ability to take directions."

"Next time, when I'm not in a hurry. I'd like to see you behind the wheel of my car."

Inside the car, Rashad leaned over to kiss her, took her hand in his and they headed toward enchantment.

Chapter 6

Rashad let Michelle in the front door with a breath of anticipation and turned on the light in the foyer. His Yorkie had been waiting for him, and the dog got to Michelle before he did, yelping and jumping up to her knee and wagging his tail, excited for a visitor.

"I'm sorry." Rashad lifted the little thing with one hand to stop its hyper assault. "This is Shaka Zulu, my Yorkshire terrier. He's very happy to meet you. I know. It's kind of Paris Hilton to have a tiny dog, but he was all alone at the shelter. No, actually, he was with a whole litter. He was just cute. Tell Michelle it's Taye Diggs or Bruce Willis to have you—manly men. Okay, yes. I talk to the dog. I think you and Andre will have fun when you meet."

Michelle was laughing fit to pee herself and hugging her middle. When she stopped, she managed to say between gasps, "And his name is Shaka Zulu?"

"Yes, quite. Shaka to friends."

And she was off again with laughter, hopping up and down.

"It's okay, Shaka. She's a mean lady."

"Aw. No, I'm not. He's precious." Michelle rubbed Shaka's head.

"Let me put him in the den so he'll go to sleep."

"Okay."

When Rashad came back from upstairs, he found that Michelle had turned on the living room light and was looking around. She wasn't interested in the leather sofas or the Amish wood or the plush carpet, however. She was looking at his artwork, which was all by relatively unknown local artists and all original.

She glanced his way when she heard him.

"You have some great pieces here."

"Thank you. I add a piece now and again, whenever I find something that inspires me or just something that I like. I hope to have some pieces of yours soon."

Rashad moved behind her and looked briefly at the image before Michelle, seeing it with new eyes. But then he was enticed by the artwork that was standing right in front of him.

Michelle had on a yellow peasant top and a matching crinkle skirt with one-inch heels and a yellow sweater. He had never seen her in a dress before, and it made him want to touch her all over.

He wrapped his arms around her, leaving one at her waist and moving the other to her breasts. When her nipples tensed and her body leaned into his embrace, he knew that she was beginning to feel again what they had felt in the theater. He hadn't stopped feeling it.

He lowered his lips to her ear and heard her suck in her breath, and when he lowered them to her neck, continuing to knead her breasts, her breathing became quicker and more labored. He wanted to turn her around and carry her upstairs, but he wanted her to be ready and to go because she wanted him, too.

Rashad took his hand from her waist and moved it down her outer thigh and up her inner thigh until he reached her center. He moved his palm over the weave of her skirt until her buttocks bucked against his groin, pressing against his rigid member and shooting a hot wave through his center. That was where she liked it. He rubbed his fingers over that place until she moaned.

"What are you doing to me?" she asked, but he couldn't speak.

When he stopped, he felt her wince, but he only stopped a moment, long enough to lift the hem of her skirt and replace his fingers over her thick mound. Her legs parted slightly, granting him access, and as his finger slid over her panties and he felt the slick moisture there, he lifted his head from her neck, clutched at her breasts and groaned.

Rashad moved his hands between Michelle's thighs until her throat came alive and her hips gyrated from the pressure of his fingers. The oscillation of her buttocks against his swollen peak sent sparks through him and made him ready. So did her moaning and thrusting.

"What are you doing to me?" she said again.

Her sounds and movements were leading him toward the edge. But he knew he couldn't reach that point, not before he knew what it was to please this woman.

Just when he thought he couldn't stand any more, Michelle turned to him, pressing her body against his and burying her face against his shoulder to catch her breath.

When she lifted her face to his, the passion he saw in her eyes filled him with pride and made him smile.

She reached up to his face and pulled it to hers, then gently pressed her lips to his. Her kiss was soft at first, almost hesitant. As she became lost in the moment, her lips parted and let in his searching tongue. Her hand crept down his chest between them, as if unsure. He pulled one arm from around her body and found her breast again. Now her hand became certain, raking his chest and moving down his abdomen to the crest in his slacks. He knew she was going to take hold of him, yet he wasn't prepared for the fire that licked through his sex and the long moan that he poured into her mouth.

He moved his hand down to her skirt again, lifted it and tugged her panties aside, fighting his own need to explode. His fingers circled her moist meadow. She thrust against them and winced. When his fingers kneaded the small crown between her inner lips, she clutched the front of his shirt and let out a series of sobs.

She had ceased to touch him, but the flame she'd lit still moved through him, and he wanted to make her feel that flame. He continued to knead her as she moaned. And then her breaths became short. Her thrusts became hard and she sobbed out his name while her body bucked, bringing her over the edge.

When it was over, Michelle fell forward into his arms, and Rashad had to catch her against his chest.

After a few moments, her eyes flew open, and she looked at him as if shocked by what she'd done.

"That was beautiful, Michelle."

He pulled her close and held her against his body.

"What did you do to me?"

"What do you mean?"

"I've never felt that way before."

Perplexed, Rashad breathed in the scent of her hair and asked, "Have you ever had an orgasm before?"

She was quiet for a moment, and when she spoke it was against his neck.

"Not with anybody else and not like that."

"Not with anybody else? But by yourself, you mean?"

She nodded her head.

But weren't you married? He wanted to ask that question but didn't need to. He understood what she meant. And what she meant raised too many other questions for him to ask right then.

When she had gotten her wind back, Michelle lifted her head.

"Are we finished?" she asked and smiled.

"I hope not."

"Where is your bedroom?"

In answer, Rashad lifted Michelle in his arms and carried her up the steps to the master bedroom. He laid her on his California king and turned on the lamp next to the bed.

The dim light outlined Michelle's features, showing Rashad a woman whose face seemed always on the verge of a smile. His mind raced from thought to thought. Here was a woman who hadn't been pleased by her own husband, by anyone. And he wanted to be the one to please her that way and always.

He pulled a condom out of his drawer and stepped back to the bed. Michelle was taking off her clothes, and he watched her, mesmerized, before he snapped to attention and started to take off his.

With her clothes off, she opened her arms to him in a gesture that filled him with a possessive desire. He went to her, but he didn't enter her arms. He coaxed her back down to the bed.

"Let me kiss your body."

"You've done enough for me. It's your turn."

"It's our turn—together."

Michelle rolled her eyes, and he chuckled, but she acquiesced, giggling.

Rashad started with her lips, slowly. He wanted to take his time with this woman. He moved down to her breasts, which were all that he had imagined, and she finally stopped trying to pull him down to her. She relaxed on top of his comforter and began to enjoy what he was doing.

He kept his lips and tongue working against her breasts. After a little while, Michelle began to stir and a soft whimper escaped her. Rashad was elated that she was getting turned on again, and every signal of it engorged his manhood even more.

After some time of his lips against her breasts, she began to writhe on the bed, and when Rashad saw her hand move down between her own legs, he almost lost control.

He took her hand away, lowered himself between her thighs and licked her lips. Her back arched off the bed, and she moaned. Her sounds of pleasure were his muse and his music, making his member leap.

"What are you doing to me?" Michelle asked for the third time.

"Loving you," Rashad answered before dipping his tongue into her wetness.

Michelle cried out in pleasure, and her body twisted on the bed. He tilted his head and gently sucked her tender bud into his mouth. Michelle cried out again, and her knees began to tremble. He tilted his head down and returned his tongue to her wet cave. He alternated between the gentle sucking and the shallow dipping until she was crying out in short, rhythmic puffs of air. Damn, he loved giving pleasure to this woman.

It took Rashad a minute to realize that Michelle was tapping on his shoulder and calling his name to get his attention. He raised his head, and she tugged him upward. He followed her direction.

She took several deep breaths before she kissed his lips, and when she settled back, she gazed into his face.

"Rashad," she said, "come inside me."

He smoothed her hair down, startled by the tenderness that was moving inside him for this woman.

"I wasn't finished what I was doing. I love giving you pleasure that way. Let me satisfy you that way. You've never had that, have you?"

She shook her head.

"Then let me give you that."

"Next time. You said that this was *our* turn." She moved her hand down to his leaping member, drawing its moisture. "And I want you inside me."

Under the spell of her hand and captured by the plea in her voice, Rashad was spinning out of control.

His fingers roved down her body, and he began to knead her sex with his palm, wanting her ready, knowing it had been a long time for her. He wanted to please her this way, too, if he could.

When her hips thrust against his palm, signaling her readiness, Rashad found the condom packet he'd lost on the bed, slid on the slick disk and positioned himself between Michelle's legs.

Just when he thought he was in control, she slipped her hand between them and gripped him, guiding him to her entrance. He began to move inside her inch by swollen inch, giving her time to adjust to his presence. She was so tight, so warm, so wet. He gritted his teeth to keep his composure, to keep going slowly, gently. Once he was inside, he paused.

"Are you okay?" he asked. "I know it's been a while."

"I'm okay," she said. "You feel good inside me."

Michelle pulled his head down and claimed his lips, and he began moving slowly inside her, letting her get used to his movement.

She tilted her hips and pressed her fingers into his back, drawing him farther inside and lighting his passion.

She rocked with him, thrusting upward onto his body, making him groan.

"Faster," she commanded, and he began to plunge inside her. Her moan filled his mouth, and her sex clung to his. Her fingers raked his back, and her body heaved upward against him.

Rashad choked back a groan, trying to retain his control. He brought one of his hands from beneath Michelle and began to play with her breasts as he rocked inside her. Her murmur filled his mouth; her sex contracted around him. She started to thrust harder against him.

"Rashad," she called.

"Yes. Anything."

"Don't stop what you're doing to me."

"I won't," he said. And now he had to keep his promise, and the beauty of this woman made that a difficult thing to do.

Rashad closed his eyes, ran his thumb over the peak of the nipple under his hand and continued his seduction, so wanting to please her this way.

When she cried out and her fists pounded his chest, he knew she was near the end. He moved his hand from her chest and pressed his thumb over her sex. She cried out again and pummeled against him. Her womanhood gripped his sheathed flesh tighter. She called his name, and he felt the first waves of her contraction ripple along his sex; her body began to shudder.

Hearing his name from her raspy throat pushed Rashad over the edge, where he had been dangling for so long, and he groaned as he fell along the precipice. He gripped her hips and locked himself inside her, his body going rigid at the crest of an upward plunge. He called her name as the flood within him broke, throbbing through the channel.

Rashad felt Michelle squeeze herself around him, drawing him on, milking him. He opened his eyes in surprise as he poured into her.

After he caught his breath, Rashad lowered himself next to Michelle and pulled her into his arms.

"Thank you," she said.

"Thank you?"

"I— Thank you."

Michelle nestled her forehead against his cheek, and he ran his hand along her nude figure as they both quieted. As the sound of their breathing became slow and steady, questions circled Rashad's mind. What the hell had her husband been doing for those years if he was holding a woman so clearly unused to being satisfied with a man? And what did it mean that he was determined to be the one to satisfy her?

He rubbed her hair, and she hummed briefly. She was falling asleep.

He returned his fingers to her side, tracing her silhouette. She was so different from what he thought he wanted. Beautiful, yes. But his expectations hadn't included a woman with a past and a child, a woman with a wild youth and an ex-husband. Even her beauty didn't fit the paradigm that he'd created for himself. Instead of the sleek, glossy, high-heeled, high-powered image he had of his ideal match, she had translucent eyes and a face that always seemed on the verge of a smile. She was a mixture of a little bit of feisty and a lot of down-home sweetness.

He kissed her forehead and pulled her naked body against his. Regardless of the image in his head, he couldn't deny the tenderness he felt for this woman. Soon he would have to get up, wash off, put them under the covers. But for now he just wanted to feel her naked body against his.

He was sure that when they had started the evening, neither had known they would end up making love on his California king. Now he lay next to her naked, sleeping figure. This woman just put him at ease.

Chapter 7

Michelle closed the book for Introduction to Public Relations and checked the PowerPoint slide at the front of the room to make sure she had taken all the notes. While the professor was wrapping up, her mind had skipped ahead. It was Wednesday, and after getting home, after getting Andre something to eat and after getting him to the sitter, she would be going to her art class.

Rashad would be there, and it would be the first time she'd seen him since their night at his place. They wouldn't be doing anything after class tonight, but they could still talk at her car, and she would still follow him to Greenbelt, even though she knew the way by now.

Michelle heard the faint ring of the Founders Library clock tower and started packing up.

The student in front of her turned around. "Do you have good notes from last week? I was out."

"Yeah," Michelle answered. "Give me your email, and I'll scan them for you."

"Great. Do you want to put together a study session for the midterm?"

"No. I work, so I can never make the time."

The other student seemed disappointed, and Michelle wondered how many times she'd been "out." In a way, Michelle was glad to be an older student. She knew what she wanted and that she didn't have time or money to waste. She didn't goof off or skip classes; she couldn't afford to.

She took the page the other student handed to her.

"I'll email you by tomorrow night."

"Thanks."

Michelle slung her backpack over her shoulders and headed for Georgia Avenue to walk to the Metro, not bothering to wait for the campus shuttle. There was precious little parking on campus, so she had to park at the Metro and take the train in.

After she got Andre from his preschool and settled him at the table to do his homework, she went to change her clothes. She still had on her uniform from her shift at the coffeehouse that morning and wanted something more comfortable (and more attractive) to wear to class.

She was in her room stripped down to her underwear when her phone rang. Without giving it a thought, she picked up the receiver and said, "Hello?"

"I don't need your hello."

Michelle placed the voice immediately and crossed her arms over her seminude body like a shield. It was Lucius, her ex-husband. Lucius Omar Vaughn. And he was drunk. His words were slow and slurred.

"What are you doing calling me?" she said. "You know you're not—"

"Don't tell me what I'm not supposed to do. You think you can get away from me? You can't."

Michelle snapped up the shirt she'd just taken off and covered herself with it.

"You can't get away from me," he said. "You can't keep my son from me, either. I pay for you. I'm paying for you both."

"I don't have to—"

"You're paid for, Miss Thing. Michelle. Michelle who thinks she's so cute. I pay for you, you whore."

"Don't call here again."

Michelle clicked off the phone, put it back on the receiver and sat on the bed with her shirt gripped to her chest.

She stared at the phone as if it had been the one talking and was about to say something else, like it was a black hole opening her universe to an alternate dimension, a nightmare world.

She waited.

The phone did not ring again.

This was a nightmare. What if Andre had answered the phone? What if he had been in the room when she answered the call? How did Lucius get her unlisted number? And if he had that, could he have other information about where she was—her address? Could he get an address from an unlisted number? What should she do now?

But she didn't do anything right away. She just sat there, staring at the phone.

"Mommy," Andre called from the dining room.

His voice sounded like a chirp. It seemed so small, so vulnerable.

"Yes, baby. What is it?"

Michelle got up and moved toward her bedroom door, ready to open it half-naked if she had to, if she had to get to her son.

"What is it, baby? What's wrong?"

"Can I have some cookies?"

Michelle let out a breath. "You go ahead, honey. They're on the counter, and I'll be right out to get you some juice."

Michelle set down the shirt that she'd been pressing to her chest, made a quick change and went to the dining room to check on Andre and get him some juice.

He was tracing a *g* in his copybook with a large pencil, completely at ease. There were two cookie wrappers next to his book, and Michelle collected them.

"How many cookies did you have?"

"Four cookies. They come two at a time."

"No more cookies right now. I'm about to get dinner."

Michelle tried to concentrate on what she was doing, but she was distracted. Lucius had her number.

After setting Andre's plate in front of him, Michelle went into the living room, where she could see him eat, and got on the computer. She pulled up her email and sent a brief note to her lawyer in South Carolina, letting her know that Lucius had called her and asking her what to do. She hit Send and let out a breath. At least she had done something, and soon she would know what she should really do. Having put something in motion, she could relax a little—but just a little. She had to be more alert now than ever.

She went to Andre and ruffled his hair.

"Is dinner okay, honey?"

"Yep."

"Eat up while I make you a snack for later. We have to go soon."

"Okay, Mommy."

Michelle got Andre to Mrs. Miller and made it to the Torpedo Factory in time for her class. Rashad winked at her and smiled when she sat down, and she couldn't help smiling back and remembering their night together—the ecstasy she'd felt, the safety of those warm arms.

"How's cute little Shaka?"

Rashad bent his head down and put on a deep bass voice. "Big, manly Shaka. Shaka Zulu." Then he laughed. "Shaka's fine. He misses you."

His mouth was open to say more, but their class started.

As usual, the hours skipped by while they were in class—taking notes, learning terms, doing exercises. But Michelle was distracted, and not just by the fact that she was sitting next to Rashad for the first time since they'd made love. There was now a cloud hanging over all that she was trying to do with her life, even this art class. And that cloud was Lucius, who now had her number.

She tied to stay focused, but part of her mind was on that call. When class was over, she could barely remember what she'd written in her notebook. She would have to read it over later.

Rashad walked her to the parking lot, and they kissed at her car, but she said she couldn't linger.

They didn't make plans for the weekend because she had to study for a midterm on Monday in her communications law class, and he had a work project due, but they made plans to talk on the phone, to see each other in class and to set up something for the next weekend.

Michelle followed him to Greenbelt, retrieved a sleeping Andre from the sitter, tucked him in, had a bite to eat and began to pull out her clothes for the next day.

She glanced at the phone. The call hadn't left her mind, and now the phone itself had come to stand for the enemy.

She went into the living room and checked her email. Nothing yet. She changed and got in bed. Maybe it was a onetime thing. Maybe it was just because he was drunk. Maybe that would be the end of it. But she knew Lucius, and she was hoping against hope, against the weight of her experience with him.

She heard from her lawyer the next day. Her lawyer wanted more information so that she could file a complaint on Michelle's behalf and alert the police to his violation of the court order that had been issued after their divorce.

A week went by without further incident—but only a week.

The next Wednesday when she got home, it wasn't the phone but the mail that assaulted her. She got an unsigned letter. Her address was typed, and inside was one of those kinds of things you see in detective movies, where the serial killer cuts out words from different magazines and glues them down. But it said just what Lucius had said to her: "You can't get away. You can't keep him from me. I pay for you."

She got the real message being sent: he had her address now, and he wasn't afraid to use it. Michelle knew he could show up at any moment, court order or not. She didn't know if he would have the nerve to risk being arrested, and she didn't care about anything that concerned her. It was the second line that bothered her most: "You can't keep him from me."

The black hole bordering her universe had just expanded. Tears of anguish and frustration formed at the corners of her eyes and slid down her cheeks.

Michelle wiped the wet streaks from her face and shoved the letter under her spread of bills when Andre came in.

"Mommy, I can't get this in my backpack. Mrs. Miller said I could bring Mr. Wiggles to sleep with."

Andre's stuffed bear, which was almost as big as he was, protruded butt-first from his bag full of toys and games.

Michelle smiled weakly at her son and got up to take hold of his backpack.

"Why don't you just carry Mr. Wiggles?"

"Then people will see."

"Oh." Michelle got it. He was too big to be seen with a bear but still wanted to sleep with it. "Hmm. I know." She went to her closet and started digging around. "I have one of those bags that tightens with a rope and goes over your back. I think he'd fit in there. Is that okay?"

She got Andre situated, sent another email to her lawyer, left Andre with the sitter and made it to her class. But she was a bit unhinged that evening. At her car, she finalized plans with Rashad for the weekend and turned to get in. He pulled her back.

"You okay tonight?"

"Yeah, just distracted. Nothing that we need to talk about," she added to cut him off.

"I want an update on you this weekend," he said and drew her in for a long kiss.

At first Michelle couldn't give herself to the moment, but as Rashad's lips pressed against hers, they stilled her. Then she felt his tongue move into her mouth. She pressed her body against his and felt him tighten his grip on her back. As his mouth explored hers, she could feel the heat rising in him, and his inflamed manhood pressed against her hip. She murmured, wanting to feel it against her sex, and her hips tilted toward him. As if reading her mind, he cupped her bottom and brought her flush against him. A brief moan escaped her throat, and wetness flooded her center.

When they broke the kiss, she was flushed and breathy.

"Do I still have it going on?" Rashad teased.

In response, Michelle only rapped his chest with the back of her hand and smiled.

He pulled back. "Don't forget. I want an update on you this weekend."

"Okay," she said, but she was already wondering if she should still go out with him considering what was going on.

"Promise?"

"Okay."

And Michelle kept her promise, at least partly.

When he picked her up, she was wearing an African-print dress that Regina had given her for her last birthday and her African mudcloth wrap. Rashad planned to show Michelle another part of the city, and, on their way, she updated him on her classes, how she had done on her midterms, Andre (who was at the sitter's for the rest of the day) and how far she'd gotten on the project for a women's center logo that she wanted to add to her portfolio.

He listened to everything. Then he said, "And so what was really going on on Wednesday?"

Michelle sighed. "I thought I'd gotten around that."

Rashad shook his head and smiled.

"Well, nothing I want to talk about—just a bit of disturbing news in the mail."

He waited, but she didn't go on. He had her hand, and he lifted it to his lips before rubbing her fingers.

"You know you can tell me anything."

"I know."

He squeezed her hand. "Do you really know?" he insisted.

"Yes," she said. "I know."

"There's no part of you I don't want to know."

He lifted her fingers to his lips again.

"Okay," she said. After a couple moments of quiet, she shot the question back at him. "What about you? Give me an update."

He told her how his project for work had turned out, what he was working on next and how Shaka was doing, and then they pulled into the crescent of parking spaces at the Tidal Basin.

"I've seen the monuments," Michelle said. "Well, I've driven by the monuments."

They both chuckled.

"Yes," Rashad countered, "but have you gone out in one of the paddleboats at the Tidal Basin?"

"What?"

"Today is a water-themed day."

"I don't swim well," Michelle said.

"Yes, that's why everybody has to wear those big orange life vests."

"You're kidding, right?"

"I kid you not."

Michelle looked down at herself. "I have on a dress."

Rashad followed the line of her gaze. "I don't see the problem."

"I'm not getting out of this, am I?"

Both of them chuckled.

They had a fun time paddling the basin for an hour, and then they walked the basin a bit to see the cherry blossom trees even though they weren't in bloom. They continued their walk up to the National Mall and into the National Gallery of Art Sculpture Garden.

Michelle was delighted by the works.

"Oh, look at these."

They stopped in front of piece called *Thinker on a Rock,* by Barry Flanagan. It was an obvious homage to Rodin's *The Thinker,* which had a man sitting on a rock. This one was a big bunny sitting on a rock. Michelle and Rashad were amused when they saw it.

After the Sculpture Garden, Rashad drove them to the waterfront in D.C. He had booked them seats on a *Spirit of Washington* dinner cruise along the Potomac. Michelle was overwhelmed.

"You didn't have to go through all this."

"It was no trouble. This way, you can see some of D.C., and we can eat while you're doing it."

They boarded on time, waited on the deck for push off and went below just after that to be seated for dinner. Rashad got them a seat by the window.

"Keep a lookout. This is the city you never go out to see."

Michelle was still stunned by the whole thing.

"This is expensive," she said. "We could have done something free."

Rashad laughed. "We'll do free stuff, as well. Which reminds me, next weekend is the Kennedy Center with my family. I'll get you the details."

"Your family?"

"Yes, and pay no attention, none whatsoever, to what any of my brothers say about me."

Rashad laughed, but Michelle was suspicious.

"They're your brothers. They probably know you quite well."

"Okay. You might not get to come along."

She put on a pout, and he grinned. Then he got serious. "I really want you there."

"Okay."

"But for tonight, dinner and dancing and—"

"I haven't danced since I was a wild child."

"It'll come back to you. Or not," Rashad said and laughed.

Michelle swung at his shoulder.

"Hey, don't get my dander up. Mama used to put down. You might not want to get me started. Just give me some house music."

"I don't know that they'll have any house music here."

"What kind of music will they have?" Michelle asked.

"I don't know," Rashad said. "Probably something neither of us can dance to."

After dinner, they did dance. They did a fast set, and then the music turned slow. Rashad opened his arms, and Michelle stepped into them. He had put on the jacket that went with his suit before they boarded, and Michelle wrapped her arms around his broad shoulders. When he drew her closer, her chest grazed the front of his suit. Her nipples constricted, and she inhaled.

"I wish I could kiss your breasts," he whispered in her ear.

His voice was deep and close and sent a shiver down her back. She dipped her head to his shoulder and suppressed a murmur. This man was turning her on.

She pressed closer to him and could feel that he was turned on, as well, and that escalated her flame. She started to run her fingers along the exposed part of his neck and could feel his manhood leap against her.

"I like that," Michelle said.

"Likc what?"

"Feeling you against me."

She felt his smile against her cheek and cupped his face in her hands to kiss him.

When the music sped up again, they collected her wrap from the table and went up on deck. She spent the rest of the cruise watching the sights from the bow with Rashad's arms wrapped around her. He kept giving her small touches—his hand at her waist, his lips at her forehead, his fingers intertwining with hers. And his touches kept turning her on. She touched him, too, but she couldn't tell what effect she was having.

They went back to her place after the cruise. They clutched one another even before the door closed, her hands brushing his chest and his palms lifting her against him.

"Wait," Michelle said. "Let me turn on the light and check on Andre."

She flipped on the light switch and got her phone and went to the window as she dialed Mrs. Miller's number, peering into the darkness for any strange figures.

She couldn't see anything because it was too dark, and it occurred to her that she was the one who could be seen. She shut the curtain. She wondered briefly if she should have Rashad there. They should have gone to his place. But then she wouldn't be here in time to pick up Andre. She was relieved to reach Mrs. Miller and find that Andre was doing fine and was fast asleep with Mr. Wiggles.

"I'll be there on time. Am I keeping you up?"

"No, dear. I'm a night owl. I'll see you soon."

She turned around and found that Rashad had disappeared.

"We have about an hour and a half," she called.

"Okay," he answered, and she followed the sound of his voice.

She found him in her room. His jacket and shirt were off, and he was looking at her pile of papers and books for school.

"Advertising is serious business," he said when she walked in.

"Yes, it is."

Rashad turned to her bookshelf and began perusing the titles.

Michelle looked around her room. All her furniture was worn, and some of Andre's things were strewn about the floor. It certainly wasn't a boudoir for seduction, and it definitely didn't match the quality Rashad was used to.

He was looking at the photographs on the wall next to her bed. He pointed to the biggest one.

"Andre?"

"Yep, that's my sweetie."

"I hope I get to meet him soon."

He seemed earnest, and Michelle smiled, touched that he was interested enough in her that he wanted to meet her son.

She went over to where he stood, faced him and began running her hands along his chest. He still had on his undershirt, and she lifted it over his head. Then she started to kiss his neck. When she moved to his chest, he held her shoulders and pulled her upward.

"Last time you said I could finish what I was doing next time. Tonight I get to put my lips on you."

"No, we started with me last time. This time, we're starting with you."

"Last time—"

Michelle cut Rashad off by sucking one of his nipples into her mouth. She ran her hand along his chest and squeezed the other nipple between her fingers. Being in control of him this way was making her start to throb.

As she licked and tweaked his nipples, Michelle ran her other hand down the front of his pants, finding his swollen manhood. She rubbed, and his member leaped against her palm. Rashad groaned.

Michelle felt herself getting wetter and wetter, and she knew what she wanted to do.

Still caressing his manhood, she pulled her head up.

"Did you bring any protection?" she asked and held out her hand.

Rashad took his wallet out of his pocket as she undid his belt and zipper and slid her hand inside his pants. His sex pulsed against her hand, and he thrust his hips. He swallowed hard as he handed her the condom.

She pulled down Rashad's pants and backed him onto the bed. She knew that the desire in her body could be read all over her face, but she didn't care.

Once she had his pants off, she slipped the disk over him and lowered her head to follow it. It was easy giving to a man who had given so much to her before, and that made this different from everything she was used to. She wanted to make this good for him before letting him make it good for her again.

Her lips slid down his hot sex, and her tongue licked upward. He groaned and pushed gently against her mouth. She wanted to make this good.

Chapter 8

Rashad put his hands in his pockets and rocked up and down on his heels. He had on one of his more expensive suits—a two-piece navy set from Ralph Lauren—and he was standing in the lobby of the Kennedy Center across from the ticket counter.

"Don't worry, baby bro," Keith said, clapping him on the back. "She'll be here."

His parents, brothers and in-laws were milling about as they waited for Michelle, the only one who had not yet arrived.

It might not have mattered if he introduced women to his family regularly, but he never did, so that made it an occasion.

"I told you that if you play around too long, you might miss the right one," Derrick said.

Rashad dropped his head and rolled his eyes.

"Okay, okay." It was Marcus chiming in. "Let's not rattle him. She's just late."

His mother came toward him. "Here's my baby. You must be worried," she said and gave him a long hug. Over his mother's shoulder, Rashad gave his brothers a look that said "so there." Only the baby of his family could get away with that. "She'll be along."

"I know, Mom. It's okay," he said, patting his mother's back and trying to extricate himself from her doting embrace.

His father laid an arm on his shoulder. He was taller than his father, as well. "We've got time," his father said. "We'll give it another ten minutes. Come, Rosa. Let's go look at what they got on sale with the girls."

His parents headed off, and his brothers finally gave him some space.

She was standing six feet from him, and he didn't know her until she turned around.

She was stunning. She had on a close-fitting purple cocktail gown that tapered down to her knees. It was made of a shimmering material, and there was a wide ruffle at the waist that flared out over her hips and bottom. The tight upper bodice dipped into a low V at her breasts, and the back dipped down to the waist. It was crisscrossed with ribbon. Over that she wore a see-through cover-up of the same color made of a glittering gauzy material. It was longer than the gown and had a large pleat at the neck so that it opened out behind her. The cover-up also had a high collar that she wore up. This look was accented with two-inch heels and a small pocketbook.

Her hair was up on the crown of her head in a tall bun, with wisps trailing down her neck and temples. The bun had purple rhinestones in it and was surrounded at the base by a low, circular tiara made of the same stones. Her face was made up to the nines. She had a subtle band of purple eyeliner around her eyes, accenting a soft purple eye shadow with a hint of purple blush at her cheeks—flawless.

It almost wasn't her, but then there was that puckering of her cheeks that made her face always on the verge of a smile. And her smile was there, too. She was so breathtaking that his jaw dropped. He had dated gorgeous women before, but seeing Michelle this way gave a new meaning to his standards.

She rushed over to him.

"Sorry I'm late. I—"

He kissed her lightly.

"You look beautiful."

She smiled and curtsied.

"Thank you, but it's not mine. I don't own anything so fancy. Regina let me rummage through her going-out collection. I'm so glad you like it. I didn't know what to wear to the Kennedy Center, and it made me think of *The Color Purple.* I hope the show hasn't started without us. Are we locked out until intermission?"

His brothers and in-laws had seen them and started to drift over, but she was talking so fast that he couldn't make the introductions.

"I'm sorry I'm late. There are so many circles in this city! I think I got sent around every one of them—Logan Circle, Dupont Circle—"

"You went around Dupont Circle coming from Greenbelt to the Kennedy Center?" Rashad asked and started to laugh.

"Don't you start to tease me again. I took a route I knew. Wait," she said, pointing her finger at him. "Where's your mother? I'm going to put a stop to this right now."

Standing behind her, his brothers started to laugh; Keith whooped in glee. She turned and noticed the row of well-dressed men and looked back to him, clamping her mouth shut apologetically.

He smiled and took her arm, and they stepped toward his brothers.

"Michelle, this is my older brother Keith, the one making a fool of himself by hooting in the theater. This is our older brother Marcus and his partner, Trevor. And this is our older brother Derrick, the sedate one."

Michelle had clasped each of their hands in turn, and now she got a quizzical look in her eyes.

She turned to them. "Is this one the baby of the family? Are you the youngest? That explains a lot. And Mama spoiled him rotten, didn't she?" His brothers were nodding in assent, and Keith even clapped.

"She's got your number," Keith said.

"Well, I don't know if Mama will be of any help at all—not with her baby."

"I'll stand in for her," Derrick said. "What's he doing?"

"He keeps teasing me because I don't know D.C. that well. I work. I go to school. I don't drive a tour bus."

"No, no," Rashad said to defend himself. "She's directionally challenged. Challenged, I tell you."

Derrick began to wag a finger at him, and Rashad knew a brotherly lecture was coming. Michelle and his other brothers were already chuckling.

"Rashad, you need to respect this young woman, or I'll whoop your behind. I—"

Rashad protested heartily. "You're not hearing me. Challenged, I say."

Michelle pointed toward Derrick. "I like you already. You," she said, looking back at him, "you need to mind." Then she laughed.

"Don't gang up on me with them," Rashad warned. "They do it all the time. It's just pure jealousy."

"You might need some ganging up on. You know—" Michelle turned to his brothers "—I think I need to get some info from you guys."

"Oh, no. No, no, no." Rashad shook his head, but he knew he was up against a losing battle.

"We'll be happy to fill you in," Marcus said.

"Whatever you want to know," Keith added.

"Well, let's start with why this one—"

"No, no. Look at the time." Rashad tapped on his watch. "We better go find our parents and your wives before we really are late."

Michelle pouted for a second and then conceded.

"Rain check," Keith said. "But soon."

"I'm so sorry I'm late," Michelle said to the guys.

"Don't worry about it. You're here." Rashad touched her back as they ambled toward the gift stand.

"Look at this place," Michelle said. "It's amazing. Look at how high the ceiling is."

"There's a promenade outside, as well," Rashad said. "I'm sorry we won't have a chance to walk it this time."

"I saw masqueraders on the way here," Michelle said. "People are in costumes already."

"I know," Marcus said. "Halloween may be tomorrow, but the festivities are starting tonight."

"So will the sirens downtown," Keith added.

"What are we going to see?" Michelle asked.

"The Dance Theatre of Harlem," Trevor said.

They found Rashad's parents and sisters-in-law at the gift stand outside their theater, looking at posters and art.

"Oh, I love those." Michelle was looking at the posters of the Dance Theatre of Harlem. "I love art that captures the human body in such beautiful motion."

"Composition and design," Rashad said.

He noticed Michelle go quiet as they approached his parents.

He rubbed her shoulder and pulled her closer to whisper in her ear. "It's okay. I won't tell them about your wild younger days."

She whispered back, "You better not, or I'll tell Derrick."

Rashad chuckled as they stepped up to his parents, but Michelle didn't. She put on a pensive smile.

"Mom, Dad, this is Michelle. Michelle, these are my parents, down from Baltimore."

"Good evening. I'm so sorry I'm late. I left on time, but—"

Rashad started to laugh, and Derrick gave him a light clap on the back of the head from behind.

"I'm sorry," Michelle repeated.

"No problem. Glad you're here," his father said, shaking Michelle's hand.

His mother approached Michelle, held Michelle's face in both of her hands and looked at her closely.

"You're a darling. Come meet the girls."

His mother tugged Michelle away from him and drew her toward his two sisters-in-law. Rashad couldn't hear what they were saying, but in a few moments the women's laughter reached his ears.

Rashad's father put a hand on his shoulder.

"She's a pretty woman, but mind you, looks don't do it all."

"I know, Dad. She's more than a pretty picture."

Derrick heard that and gave his younger brother a long, firm stare.

"You might be settling down after all."

Rashad, who always balked at his older brothers' mandate to settle down, looked over at Michelle, who beamed like an angel in her shiny wrap, and he considered it.

"You never know," he replied. "You never know."

Derrick raised an eyebrow.

The lights dimmed and then came back up, their signal to head inside. Rashad took Michelle's hand when she approached and gave her a ticket for the seat next to his.

"Do I have time to call and check on Andre? I need to."

They hung back as Michelle made a brief call, and then they joined the others at their seats.

Michelle seemed enamored with the performances. They did one piece in which they used long bands of blue cloth to represent water, raising them and lowering them as the action called for it. They did pieces to spirituals, blues, funk—some of everything.

Rashad, in contrast, found that he was enamored with Michelle—the way she moved with the music, the way the images seemed to inspire her, the way she looked in that purple gown.

He was wondering about his prior aspirations and assumptions. This woman wasn't a high-powered lawyer in a tight-fitting skirt, but she was gorgeous and fun and sweet. And if he had thought she didn't fit the sleek image of his ideal mate that he carried around in his mind, she had corrected him tonight. She had shown him that she was that beautiful, too, and she had shown him that his image could be put on and taken off. It was that superficial. There had to be heart underneath it to make it count for anything.

Rashad was startled when the lights went up for intermission. He hadn't been paying attention to the show.

Michelle leaned toward him.

"I'm going to call home again before it gets too late."

"Is everything all right? Is Andre okay?"

"Yes, yes. I just want to check."

Rashad stood and sidled with Michelle to the aisle, then waited while she climbed the steps. She seemed to be checking in a lot. Maybe she'd been watching too many Halloween specials. He lingered in the aisle and caught Derrick staring at him. Rashad nodded and smiled.

You never know, he thought. *You never know.*

He took two steps at a time when he saw her at the top

on her way back, and he gave her his arm so that she could steady herself in her heels, but she didn't really need it.

Back in their seats, she stretched her shoulders and let her head fall back for a moment.

"Tired?"

"No. Well, a little. But I'm loving this. And your family is great."

"They are."

"Are we doing anything after this? I have to be home before I turn into a pumpkin."

Rashad chuckled.

"I think it was the coach that turned into a pumpkin."

Michelle nodded.

"My parents are staying over with Derrick. We meet up again tomorrow for brunch. Can you come? Maybe bring Andre so he can meet my nieces and nephews?"

"That would be great, but I have to work, and then I have to study. If I had known sooner—"

"No, I know. I should have thought about it earlier, but I didn't know about the brunch myself until yesterday. As for tonight, we're on our own. I don't know what time the show ends, but maybe you want to get something to eat, or I can fix us something simple at home."

"Home sounds good."

They smiled at one another and joined hands, and like magic, the lights dimmed.

After the second half of the show, Rashad's family lingered briefly in the main atrium of the Kennedy Center so that all could say their good-nights. Then Michelle followed Rashad home to his house, where he put Shaka in the spare room and started on their late-night snack.

A long counter separated his kitchen from a little breakfast nook, and Michelle sat at the counter while he made them sandwiches. It didn't seem quite fitting with the gown she had on, and part of him wanted to take her someplace fancy where they could finish the night. But the larger part of him wanted her to himself and to end the night with her in his arms.

They heard a rumble from the street, and Michelle hopped down from her stool.

"What was that?"

"It sounded like a trash can. Maybe a dog or a deer. We get those here sometimes."

"Could you check it?"

"It's probably nothing, and my alarm is set."

"I'll check it."

Michelle bounded toward the door leading from the kitchen to the backyard.

"Whoa. Hold up. Let me check it."

Rashad went out back and found a large dog rummaging through an overturned garbage can belonging to his next-door neighbor. The dog had a tag, so he drew it into his backyard and shut the gate. He could call the animal people in the morning. When he returned to the kitchen, Michelle had her back to him. She was on the phone with her sitter. All seemed to be well on the other end, so he went back to their meal.

When Michelle turned around, she jumped.

"I didn't hear you come back in. You startled me."

"I'm sorry—you were on the phone. I didn't want to disturb you. It was just a dog in my neighbor's garbage can. I put it out back. I'll make a call or two in the morning."

She let out a deep breath and went back to the stool.

She seemed just a little jumpy. Yes, too many Halloween specials. Rashad thought he knew what would relax her, but he wanted to feed her first.

They had their sandwiches in the living room, and then Michelle asked for some music.

"What do you feel like hearing?"

"Teddy Pendergrass or Barry White or—"

"Luther Vandross?"

"Yes," she said. And when he had put the CD in the changer, she held out her arms to him. "Dance with me."

Rashad went to her and wrapped his arms around her waist as they began swaying to the music. She murmured when he rubbed her back, so he took her hair down and spread his fingers over her scalp.

When he was finished, he held her again, and she wrapped her arms around his shoulders, folding herself along his body and resting her head against his.

"Thank you," she said softly.

It was peaceful between them for a long while.

When she stirred, it was to take off her cover-up and run her hands along his arms and shoulders. Then she tilted her head up to claim his lips. In two-inch heels, she was almost his height, and she angled toward him, grazing herself against his manhood until he had to suck in his breath.

Rashad possessed her mouth with his and ran his hands over the silky fabric of her gown everywhere he could reach. When he reached her breasts, she made a small sound, and then she pressed her palm between them until it covered his sex. The fire was building in both of them.

As beautiful as her dress looked on her, Rashad wanted it off. He felt along the crisscrossed ribbon at the back and stopped.

"You're going to have to help me with your dress," he said.

Michelle turned around and pressed her buttocks back against his groin until his hips rocked forward. Then she stepped away from him and lifted her hair.

"Pull the bow and then loosen the lacing."

He did.

"Now part the ruffle and undo the little zipper in the back."

He did, and she slid the gown from her shoulders and

shimmied out of it. It fell to her ankles, and she stepped out of it. She was left in a black lace bra and panties, garters holding up her thigh-high stockings, and black heels. And the image of Michelle this way was one of the most erotic things Rashad had ever seen.

He opened her bra and stooped to lick the cusps of her breasts, and her hips angled closer. He moved his hand between her legs to knead the thin black strip that separated him from her sex. It was already wet. She moaned as he aroused her. When he dropped to one knee and ran his tongue over the slick mesh of her panties, Michelle arched her back, threw her head back and cried out.

Frustrated with the obstacle, he pulled aside the moist black patch and sucked her womanhood into his mouth. She cried out again, thrusting along his mouth, and began to gasp for air. Then he joined his suckling with a hand upon her breast. Her fingers dug into his shoulders as she tried to steady herself, and soon she cried out again and again, her body going taut with climax. How he loved pleasing this woman.

Rashad held Michelle's thighs to keep her from toppling backward. When she was steady, he stood, pushed the hair back from her face and kissed her gently on the lips.

"That was so beautiful," he said. "You're beautiful."

"I don't know how you do that to me. Thank you."

"Are we finished?"

"Not by a long shot," she said, tugging him upstairs.

In his bedroom he pulled out a condom. She pulled off his clothes, backed him onto the bed and put the condom on him. She undid her garter and pulled off her panties.

Then without a word, she climbed onto the bed, straddled his thighs and lowered herself onto him.

Rashad moaned as she settled on his hips, and then he moaned as she bent forward and began to rake her breasts along his chest, riding him.

He was getting lost in sensations, but he wasn't completely lost yet. He was wishing that she could make it to the brunch tomorrow. He couldn't stop thinking about this woman.

Chapter 9

Michelle took Sharon from Regina's arms.

"Aw. She's fast asleep. I got her."

"Are you sure?" Regina asked.

"I'm sure," Michelle whispered. "You go get ready."

"You don't have to whisper. Once she goes down like this, it would take an earthquake to wake her. And when she's ready to wake up, hold your hat down."

"Don't worry," Michelle said. "That will change."

"I'll be back soon," Regina said.

It was Friday night, and Nigel and Regina were going to a business opening for one of Nigel's clients at the accounting and investing firm where he worked. Regina and Nigel had been married for a year and a half now, and Sharon was only twelve months. Michelle would be sitting for them, and she and Andre were staying the night at their house in Maryland.

The next day, she had to work, and then she had a date with Rashad—her second in as many weeks, though there was no way to top the Kennedy Center or what had come afterward. Andre would be spending the day with Nigel and Regina until she came to pick him up.

In a little while, Regina came out wearing a red gown. "How does this look?" she asked.

"It looks fabulous. What kind of business is opening?"

"It's a produce market up on Connecticut Avenue. This is the second business opening this month, and this is not Nigel's major work. I'm glad he's doing so well, but he's keeping me busy."

"You have a life," Michelle said. "Enjoy it."

"I know, but now that the studio has started to catch on, I have lots of my own work to do."

"Your studio is taking off. Enjoy that, too. But two pieces of advice. One, hire help—you deserve it. Two, intern art students. The city's full of universities with students who could learn from you and take a load off your shoulders."

Regina's jaw dropped. "I never thought of that. They're both good ideas. Are you sure you shouldn't be a business major?"

"No, I'm more art than administration. I'm in the right place."

"I know you are," Regina said. "And since we're on you, how are things going with that handsome man you're seeing?"

Michelle felt her cheeks flush and couldn't stop herself from smiling.

"Uh-huh. I see." Regina had come to sit next to Michelle and now nudged her with a shoulder.

"It's going okay."

"Just okay?"

"Better than okay."

Regina stood. "You know you're going to tell me more

before you leave here. But right now, I should go do my hair before Nigel gets home."

Not long after Regina went upstairs, Nigel came in from work in a three-piece tailored suit, already ready to go out for the evening.

"Hey, cousin," Michelle said.

"Hey," he returned and then came to hug her. He went to Sharon's crib and lightly fingered her hair. "Where's Reggie?"

"Finishing her hair."

Regina came down, putting on her earrings. Nigel went to her and wrapped her in his arms for a long, sensuous kiss. The love and affection they shared was enviable, and it made Michelle wistful.

Andre came down from the guestroom with a book in his hand.

"Mommy," he called.

"Shh," Michelle cautioned. "Come, honey. We can't yell when your cousin Sharon is asleep."

Michelle had her books and notes spread open on the coffee table in front of her, and she put the book she was reading aside to take Andre up on her lap. She squeezed him to her chest and kissed the top of his head.

"Can we watch a movie before we read?"

"Mommy's going to read, but if you go get the movie you want to see, we can put it on down here where I can see you, and you can watch with the volume real low. Okay?"

Andre nodded and scooted off her lap to run upstairs.

"I'll put it in before we go," said Nigel, taking up Regina's wrap.

Regina came over to give her some instructions on Sharon, but Michelle beat her to it.

"The bottles are in the fridge. I know where the diapers are. You'll set the alarm before you go. Numbers are on the fridge."

Regina put a hand on her hip. "Well, okay, Miss I Got It Going On."

"But I do. I got this covered."

Regina hugged her as Nigel put the movie in for Andre. Michelle watched Nigel set the alarm, and then both were gone.

Michelle relaxed a bit for the first time in almost a week. After what had happened earlier in the week, her nerves were frayed, and being away from home in a place that was secure felt like a bath of warm water.

Since the letter from Lucius, there had been a couple of other calls. The last one was a week ago, the night before the Kennedy Center. Lucius had been sober that time, but just as disparaging. He rattled off the same nonsense he had the first time and then hung up on her when she started to tell him to leave her alone. She sent emails to her lawyer after each call, and they were supposed to be checking her phone records to trace them to Lucius. But he was probably too smart to call from his own phone.

She was tired of being rattled by him. Back in the day before they were married, she had been good at letting him know what was what—not only two cents but a whole dollar's worth. Something had changed that, and she needed to change it back. She would also be getting caller ID after her next payday. She'd simply have to redo her budget and add more to the phone bill. Or she'd get rid of her landline altogether; he'd never called her cell phone.

She could ignore the calls, but she couldn't ignore what had happened Tuesday morning.

She had gotten up early to get ready for her shift at work and went into the kitchen to put on a pot of coffee and pull out something for Andre's breakfast. She'd flipped on the dining room light on her way in to shower before waking Andre, and that was when her whole day had changed.

In the middle of her dining table was a dead rat. It was

held down by a large steel two-pronged fork, the one from her barbecue set. The fork was narrow and had pierced the body of the rat, and the tines were buried in the wood of her table. She'd taken a step closer, half expecting to see maggots crawling over the dead carcass. But it was a fresh kill; the side of the rat's head was bashed in.

It could only be Lucius. The black hole had bled into her universe.

She'd glanced toward the front door and saw that it was open. He had been there—he or someone he had gotten to do this. If it was him, he was there in the D.C. area and had been in her apartment.

Michelle had dashed to Andre's room and pushed open the door.

He was there. *Thank God.*

She had gone to her room and gotten her cell phone. She had come back to Andre's room, locked them in and dialed 911 as she shook his shoulders to wake him.

Andre hadn't gotten a bath that day. She'd called Mrs. Miller to come get him before school and covered the dining table with a blanket while he was on the way out. She had handed him a cold bagel and his lunch sandwich. He was being led down the walk as the police came up it, and she'd been at her door to greet them.

She had showed them the dining table and explained about her ex-husband, Lucius. They'd been consoling but didn't seem to have enough to go on. One had asked if she had heard anything in the night. No, she hadn't. The other had asked if she'd seen who did it. Well, no, she hadn't. But she had already told them the only person it could be.

She had called work and stayed home. A detective had come and dusted for prints. The door had been pried open. No prints there. The handle of the fork. Nothing. They'd taken pictures, and she'd gotten a few on her phone, as well. In the end, a police report had been filed, and they'd said they would increase patrol of the neighborhood. Without more evidence that it was Lucius, there was nothing else they could do. Nothing.

"Could you take it away?" she had asked one of the officers.

"Yeah," he'd said, clearly thinking that this was never in his job description. "We'll get rid of it."

She had called to get the door fixed, called her building manager about the open front door, emailed her lawyer and sent her the photos she'd taken with her phone and searched online for alarm systems. She'd poured bleach over the dining table and scrubbed, but that wouldn't do. She had gone to Target, checked prices of dining tables and ended up getting a stack of plastic tablecloths. The new table would have to wait a payday or two. It was more important to get the alarm system she had decided on. She had taken their earliest installation appointment.

She'd gone back home and checked every room in case there was anything else. Then she'd showered and tried to pull herself together for when Andre came home. She'd be picking him up herself.

She had almost skipped her Wednesday evening class after that. And she'd almost canceled her date with Rashad for that weekend, as well. But if Lucius was in the D.C. area, he didn't show himself, so she'd gone on with her life as normal—at least as much as that was possible.

It was still a relief to be away from her apartment for a bit, and she was glad to babysit for her cousin. When Nigel and Regina got home, they chatted, which took her mind away from her problems for a while. She went to her job from their house on Saturday. When she got off, Rashad was supposed to meet her at the coffeehouse.

After her shift, she changed out of her work clothes into jeans. She had brought an orange turtleneck and a rust sweater to go with it, and she put on some makeup. It was nothing fancy, but they didn't have extravagant plans for the evening. She'd made it clear that she had to get home fairly early—to be ready for work the next day, she said.

Actually, she was a bit surprised that he still wanted to go out. They wouldn't be able to do anything later on if she had to be home early. He didn't seem to consider that at all; it was simply enough for him to see her. This man was recharting her world, and he didn't even seem to know it.

Michelle found Rashad loitering by the display of prepackaged coffees when she came out of the bathroom after changing.

He smiled at her and kissed her lightly on the lips.

One of her staff members was behind the counter and mouthed "hottie" at her behind Rashad's back. Michelle mouthed "back to work" at her, pointed to a customer at the counter and gave her a "you better" look.

The employee shuffled toward the customer with a smirk on her face.

"One of your subordinates?"

"I prefer *coworkers,* and yes. She thinks you're a hottie."

"I hope her boss thinks so, too."

Rashad put his arm around her, and they started out. Michelle had picked a place close by for them to have dinner.

"Have you to been to Kramerbooks & Afterwords before?"

"Only to the bookstore. My brother Marcus, the gay one, used to come here all the time when Lambda Rising was open. It was a gay and lesbian bookstore and a landmark. I can't believe they closed down."

"Oh, I hadn't heard of it."

"Before your time."

"I do know that there used to be a sex store called the Pleasure Chest up Connecticut Avenue across the street."

"Hmm. And how did you happen upon this information?"

"What are you insinuating?"

"Just wondering."

"Well, a coworker told me."

"That's innocent enough. I just wanted to be sure no one else took you there. You have...gadgets, don't you?"

Michelle poked her finger into Rashad's chest. "Don't snoop around my nightstand. My private stuff is...private."

"Ha! Now I know where to look. Note to self. Check inside Michelle's nightstand to gauge the competition."

"It's not competition."

"I know," he said, looking into her eyes. "God, you're beautiful."

"And you don't have any competition."

In response, Rashad pulled her toward him and kissed her.

They browsed in Kramerbooks while they waited to be seated. Michelle looked around them and peered out the front window of the bookstore. Rashad drew her attention back to him by cupping her chin and bringing her lips to his.

"You know, they have another one of those stores in Georgetown. I can take you one day, and we can get something to play with."

The thought of being in a sex store with Rashad made Michelle blush. "Maybe."

"Okay."

"And how do you know about these places?" Michelle asked. "Have you ever taken anybody to one?"

"Never. And everybody knows about them. I learned about them from my roommate in college. Actually, I've never used a plaything with anyone before. But I'd like to try with you."

All this talk about sex toys, along with Rashad's kisses and the way he was staring into her eyes, was making Michelle a little randy. As they were seated, she decided to turn the conversation to other topics.

It was a mild early November evening but still too cold to sit outside, and they got seats next to the window in the restaurant. Instead of changing the conversation, though, Michelle found herself staring out the window, looking for any shifty figures that might be hanging about. When she realized this, she let out a breath and shook her head. She needed to be in the moment.

Rashad had simply been looking at her.

"What's on your mind?"

"Nothing. Everything." She shrugged, not knowing what to say. She wanted to tell him about the calls, the rat, the black hole that seemed to be opening into her life, but she just couldn't. She hadn't even told Nigel and Regina. She hadn't told her mother. She hadn't told anyone. And Rashad was the last person who needed to know. Being harassed by an ex-husband didn't make her particularly appealing as a girlfriend. She not only had an ex; she had problems with him. If that didn't send Rashad flying, it would still just draw him into her problems, drag him down.

"Tell me."

There was part of her that wanted to, but reason got the better of her. She could handle it better without people knowing.

Michelle shook her head. "Nothing I want to talk about. Just a lot on my plate."

Rashad looked at her carefully. "I can imagine." He had covered her hand with his on top of the small café table, and now he was rubbing her fingers. "Maybe I can help. I can at least listen."

"It's nothing. I'm just distracted. I should call and check on Andre." She started to get up from the table but stopped.

"He's with my cousin Nigel and his wife. I'm sure he's fine." She settled back down in her seat.

Rashad was still looking at her closely. She had been anxious since the rat thing on Tuesday. She hoped it didn't show, but from the way Rashad was looking at her, it probably did. If she kept this up, she could mess things up between them. Damn her ex-husband.

"What are you thinking?" Michelle asked. "I can't tell."

"I was thinking that I want you to be able to tell me everything. I want to be part of your life. And I was thinking that you're so incredibly beautiful that I want to take you home and make love to you."

Michelle felt her face get hot. She felt herself smile.

"I know you have to get home early," Rashad added. "I'm just telling you what I was thinking."

"Okay."

For the rest of dinner, they talked about general topics—their art class getting ready to end, comments they got on their second portfolio submissions, how Andre was doing in school, what website Rashad was working on for his job.

It was basic stuff, but it drew them together, let them know something about each other's lives.

They parted at her car because she was heading to Nigel's to get Andre. She realized that she had felt safer being with Rashad than she'd felt in a while. For that reason and others, she didn't want the night to end.

She drew his head down for a final kiss, sucking in his full, moist lips. The look in his eyes when she released him made her juices flow.

"I wish I could go home with you," Michelle said. She had half a mind to call Regina and see if Andre could stay another night.

"So do I," Rashad said, "but we will. Soon."

Michelle got into her car and started toward Regina's, already missing Rashad.

Chapter 10

Rashad rotated in his chair, turning from one computer to another, backing up his work and shutting them down. He had the phone to his ear as he worked.

"Hey, beautiful."

"Hey," Michelle answered.

"I'm just finishing up some work at the office."

It was Saturday, and he had special plans with Michelle. But the web design firm also had a big client coming in on Monday, so he had come in early to take care of some details before their presentation pitch.

The agency about to hire them had sent sample photographs for use on their site. These all had to be cropped and resized. He also needed to finalize graphics for the prototype of the site that they would be showing to the clients, and this meant building drop-down menus that would be added to the last set of diagrams for several of the pages. When his changes were done, he also had to print the new web design mock-ups and leave them so they could be mounted on boards Monday morning with the rest.

He had finished all of this, and as much as he loved his work, he was ready to start the rest of his day.

"I'll be on my way in a few minutes. Are we still on?"

There was a pause, which worried him.

"Are you sure you want to do this?" Michelle asked.

"Are you kidding? I already got our tickets. We have an entry time for the aquarium and everything. What's up?"

"Nothing. I just don't want you to do this if you don't want to."

"And I wouldn't want to because…?"

"I don't know."

Rashad thought he knew the real reason Michelle was concerned.

"Look, if you're worried about your son getting attached to someone—"

"It's not that. He knows you're Mommy's friend."

"And you should know that I won't make any promises that I don't plan to keep."

"It's not that. I just want to make sure that you really want to give up your day to…do this."

"I don't want anything more."

"Okay," Michelle said. She didn't really sound convinced, but she was at least willing to suspend her disbelief. "Then we're on. But if you get there and want to end early or call it day, you say. No judgments."

"That won't happen, but, yes, I'll say."

"Deal," Michelle said.

"See you in a few."

Rashad placed the phone back in its cradle, stood, stretched and strode into the hall. The offices of the design firm were empty except for him and one other person. He was on his way to tell his coworker that he was leaving. As he padded silently on the plush carpet and rounded the mahogany reception counter, he took in the posh landscape of the lucrative little firm and reminded himself that one day he would have his own graphic and web design company. In fact, he was already well on his way.

He rapped on a door down the hall before announcing that he was on his way out. Then he deposited the printouts for mounting at the front desk and took the elevator down to the parking garage.

When he got to Michelle's, she was looking out the window of her apartment. He waved at her, and after she spotted him, she signaled for him to stay where he was. They were coming down—*they* being Michelle and Andre.

Rashad got out of his car to greet them as they came down the walkway from the apartment building. Michelle had a tentative look on her face and was holding the hand of a little boy dressed in blue corduroys, a polo shirt, a heavy pullover sweater and a scarf. She released his hand as they approached the car.

Rashad tried to imagine what he looked like to a four-year-old boy. He wore khaki pants, a white shirt and a navy windbreaker—nothing formal or stuffy. He had done that deliberately so he wouldn't seem off-putting to a child. Now he realized how much he wanted to make a good impression.

Rashad smiled, not knowing whether a hello kiss would be appropriate in front of Andre. Michelle solved his dilemma by hugging him hello and exchanging a brief, chaste kiss with him.

"Rashad, this is my son, Andre."

"Hello, Andre."

Andre hung back behind his mother, close to her leg, almost peeking out at him from behind her.

"Andre, this is my friend Rashad. Can you say hello to Rashad?"

Andre nodded without saying anything. Rashad laughed.

"Rashad is the one who brought you those toys, including the computer tablet you don't let out of your sight. Say thank you to Rashad."

"Thank you."

"You're very welcome. I brought something else to break the ice." Rashad reached into his car and drew out two books. "These are for you."

Andre came forward to take the books, and Rashad squatted and scooped Andre onto his knee. "This is one about the kinds of things we're going to see today. It's a talking book, so you can press the box on each page, and it tells you what the picture is." He let Andre press a box. He flipped some of the pages. Then he let Andre flip the pages himself and press more boxes. "You can look at this one on the way so that you're ready when we get there. You like it?"

Andre nodded.

Rashad switched the books. "This one is for you to read. It's a book made to help people learn how to read, but it has multicultural images in it so you can learn about different cultures, as well. Each frame is a letter, and when you put the letters together, you get a word, and it shows you how different cultures see that word. Do you know letters?"

Andre nodded again.

"What's this one?"

"It's a *B*."

Michelle cut in, glancing around them. "Perhaps we should finish this later. We should get going. It's a long drive. Is that okay, honey?" she asked Andre. "You can look at the books in the car."

"Okay," Andre answered.

"We'll get back to this later," Rashad said, lifting Andre onto his feet and standing up. "You guys ready?"

Michelle got Andre's booster seat from her car and got Andre settled in with his books.

As they got under way, they heard Andre pressing the buttons in the first book.

After a while, Andre asked, "What's your name?" It was obvious whom he meant.

"Rashad. And you can call me Rashad."

"Thank you, Rashad."

"You're welcome."

Andre went back to pressing the buttons in the book, so Rashad and Michelle began to talk.

"Your son is beautiful. He's so little," Rashad said.

"He is beautiful. As for little, that's perspective. You should have seen him as a baby. He was tiny. But I know what you mean. He's a child. And when you're the parent, you're all he has."

"With you as his mother, he's going to be a valuable man one day."

"That's all that matters."

After a pause, Michelle changed the subject. "I can't believe our art class is over now. It's just in time for me to buckle down and finish up my semester at Howard. Finals are in a couple weeks and final papers. But still, no more treks to the Torpedo Factory."

"Nine weeks went by quickly," Rashad said. "Especially because I got to see you every week."

"I know. I'm going to miss that."

"Can I still see you every week?" Rashad asked, touching her hand.

Michelle placed her hand in his. "I would like that."

Rashad became aware that the backseat had become quiet—no more buttons being pressed. He glanced in his rearview mirror and saw Andre craning his neck to see something out the window.

"What are you looking at, Andre?"

"An airplane. It's flying really high," the boy said.

"You like airplanes?"

"Uh-huh! I'm going to fly an airplane when I grow up."

"Okay," Rashad said. "That was need-to-know information. We should be going to the National Air and Space Museum. Have you been to the National Air and Space Museum, Andre?"

"What's that?"

"It's a big building with all kinds of planes in it, and it has all kinds of information about the history of airplanes."

"Can we go there?"

"We are definitely going there. Not today, but we'll make plans to go there soon. I'm free as early as next weekend, but we need to ask Mom."

"Can we go, Mommy?" Andre asked.

"Maybe not next weekend, but we can go." Michelle turned to Rashad. "Are you sure you want to go? I can take him on my own."

"Are you kidding? It's the National Air and Space Museum. We're going."

Michelle laughed at his fervor, and that made Rashad laugh, too.

They pulled into the parking garage at Baltimore Harbor just before noon. They parked and got to the Baltimore branch of the National Aquarium right on cue for their entry time. They had three hours to see what could be seen.

It turned out that three hours wasn't enough. They were able to spend time in the Children's Discovery Gallery, and they got to the Dolphin Discovery Amphitheater, which was next door, and the Jellies Invasion, which was on the other side. But they didn't get to the Australia exhibit, and they didn't get to the birds at all. Andre was mesmerized by the jellyfish and other invertebrates. It was like a translucent light show.

Andre let Rashad pick him up and hold him to the window to peer at the giant octopus, and he said no when Rashad started to put him down, so Rashad held him until they got to Shark Alley.

Andre's little eyes went big at the sight of sharks circling the viewing room in the huge tank.

"A shark!"

"It's so graceful," Michelle said.

"Can they get to us?" Andre asked.

"Not a chance," Rashad answered and rubbed Andre's head.

They next climbed the stairway of the circular tank to see the Atlantic Coral Reef exhibit.

"What's that?" Andre asked.

"That's a stingray," Rashad answered.

After climbing upward, they cut across to the Tropical Rain Forest exhibit, where the frogs were.

"Uh-oh," Michelle said.

"What?" Rashad asked.

"Wait for it."

"Mommy," Andre said, "can I have a frog? Please."

"There it is."

Rashad chuckled. It took them both to talk him out of it, and he did the same thing when they got to the turtles. He also asked for several of the bony fish, as well—a cardinal fish, a clown fish, a porcupine fish, even a moray eel.

They made it to the animal encounter activity, in which Andre got to touch an Australian python, and they made it to Nature's Recyclers, which showed decomposers, but they didn't get to the 4-D Immersion Film Theater.

"Mommy, I have to go," Andre said as they stood in the Harbor Overlook near the end.

"Sorry," Michelle said to Rashad, "but we need to find a—"

"Hey," Rashad responded. "Little bodies have little bladders. We should probably all go."

Michelle smiled at him.

"Oh, I have the map," Rashad said. "I'll take him, and we'll meet you there." He pointed to the page.

"Are you sure? He can come with me. I'm used to—"

"I think I got this."

"I want to go with him," Andre said, taking Rashad's hand.

Rashad was touched.

After freshening up, the group visited the gift shop. Rashad got an underwater ocean vista puzzle, a book on sea animals and a pair of pajamas for Andre. He got a jellyfish paperweight for Michelle as well as a larimar-and-silver dolphin and starfish pendant on a chain. He got himself a silk tie with turtles on it.

"These are to remember our trip since nobody remembered to take pictures."

"You don't have to spend this much," Michelle said.

"I know. It's okay."

After they left the National Aquarium, they walked along the Inner Harbor. Michelle had worn only a sweater over her blue slacks and mock turtleneck. Everything hugged her body in a way that Rashad loved, but it was a cool mid-November day. Rashad wrapped his arm over her shoulder as they strolled. Even with Andre there, she didn't seem to mind. When they separated, he took her hand, and they continued on, Andre running along ahead of them.

When it was time for dinner, they found a seafood place along the seaport.

"You know we're eating stuff we just saw swimming about," Rashad said to Andre. "These could be their cousins," he added and chuckled.

"Yuck."

Michelle swatted his arm and laughed.

"Don't terrorize my child. We don't like to think of our food walking or swimming about."

After he had finished eating, Andre scooted over to Rashad and asked him about the sea animals pictured in his new book. Rashad read bits of the text to him while Michelle finished her meal.

Outside the restaurant, Andre held out his arms for Rashad to pick him up, which Rashad did, and they rounded the Inner Harbor back to the car.

"One last stop," Rashad said. "It's a short one."

"Where to next?"

"We can't come to Baltimore without seeing the folks, and I have to give my dad his birthday present. It won't take long."

On the way to his parents' house, Michelle's face looked pained.

"What's wrong?" he asked.

"Are you sure we should go to your parents' house?" She pointed her finger toward the backseat where Andre sat.

He didn't get it.

"Of course—why not?"

She pointed her finger more adamantly toward Andre.

"And?"

"I have a son," she whispered. "What will they think?"

"They know that you have a son. After the Kennedy Center, my whole family pestered me for more details. They know you have a son and that you're divorced…."

Michelle's face crumpled again into the pained expression.

"And that's not what they want for their son."

"Michelle, they don't judge you for that. I don't care about that, and neither do they—not my parents and not my brothers or in-laws."

Michelle shook her head, clearly disbelieving. She would have to see it for herself, he thought.

"Don't worry. Trust me."

When they got to his parents' place, Rashad reintroduced Michelle and presented Andre, who had been tasked with holding the present while Rashad carried him.

Rashad put Andre down to hug his father and wish him happy birthday. Then he looked toward Andre for the present.

"Andre, are you over there shaking my dad's present?"

Everybody laughed except Michelle, who flushed a deep bronze.

"Andre," she said quickly. "You're supposed to be helping *deliver* the present."

"Okay," Andre replied, coming over to them.

Rashad cupped the little one's head and drew him over. "Andre, this is my dad, Mr. Brown."

"Hello."

Andre still held on to the box, so Rashad prodded him further. "I think you have something to give Mr. Brown."

Andre held up the small, rectangular box but apparently couldn't resist shaking it again.

Everybody laughed again, except Michelle, who got hold of the box and handed it to Rashad's father.

"I'm sorry," she said. "This is for you."

"Not a problem. Hey, little fella. Want to see what it is?"

His dad, to the consternation of Michelle, handed the box back to Andre. "You open it."

"Can I?" he asked his mother.

"You go right ahead, sweetie," Rashad's mother said.

Michelle nodded.

Andre tore at the wrapping, handing bits of paper to his mother.

It was a gold ID bracelet with his father's name engraved on it, and Andre handed it to Rashad's father, who took it, put it on and held it up.

"Now that's class. Thank you, son."

The two hugged.

"How about some cookies and milk," Rashad's mother said to Andre. "Is that okay with your mother?" She looked at Michelle.

Michelle smiled in response.

"Let's go to the kitchen."

Instead of taking Andre's hand, she took hold of Michelle's forearm, drawing her into the next room. Andre followed them.

Rashad had no idea what transpired in the kitchen, but both Michelle and his mother came back smiling in half an hour when it was time for them to go.

His mother hugged Michelle to her breast.

"I'll see you again soon."

He could see that Michelle had tears in her eyes as she hugged his mother and collected Andre in her arms.

"What happened? Why the teary eyes?"

"Nothing, we just chatted. I like your mother. She reminds me of mine."

Rashad could hear what Michelle wasn't saying and read her tears as gratitude for acceptance—real acceptance. He was glad that things had gone well.

By the time they got back to Michelle's, Andre had fallen asleep.

Michelle lifted him out of the booster seat and onto her hip; his head rested on her shoulder.

She was looking around the parking lot and jumped when Rashad put a hand on her shoulder. Now that they were back in Greenbelt, she seemed distracted again.

"I didn't mean to scare you," he said, taking Andre from her. "I got him. You get the car seat."

"Oh, thank you." She deposited the seat in her car and came back. "Would you walk us up?"

"I think I have to," he said good-naturedly. "I have the little one."

"Oh, yes."

At the door, she glanced around the hall before unlocking her door to let them in. Once inside, she led him to Andre's room, turning on the lights along the way. He couldn't tell whether she was being protective or overly cautious, but since the front door downstairs stayed open, he decided that the extra vigilance was for the best.

In the living room at the door, she accepted his good-night kiss. It was gentle at first, but once Michelle became lost in the moment, their lips became thirsty and their kiss passionate. For someone who hadn't seemed to fit his expectations, this woman was setting off his world.

Chapter 11

Michelle was counting the first register when the call came. She asked the manager of the next shift to finish for her and rushed to the Metro, to her car and to Andre's preschool, fighting back tears and a rising desperation.

She had been riding so high after Saturday at the National Aquarium. Now, three days later, and the black hole was opening around her with the potential to consume all that she loved.

The police had long since arrived by the time she got there, and in the principal's outer office, she heard one questioning Andre.

"Tell me again who he was."

"It was my daddy. He was mean. He said bad words. He said bad things about Mommy."

Michelle rushed in and scooped Andre up in her arms. The tears she had been holding back slid down her face. At least Andre was safe.

"Oh, baby. It's going to be okay. Are you all right?"

"Mommy, it was Daddy."

"I know, sweetie. It's going to be okay."

After a few moments, she let go of Andre and let him be taken to the principal's waiting room so that the officers could talk to her. She found out that a man had been seen speaking with Andre at the fence of the school's enclosed playground, and this man, according to Andre, was her ex-husband, Lucius.

"He's violating a court order that granted me sole custody and limited his visitation rights. And he's also violating a restraining order I had taken out against him," she said.

"We'll need to see the paperwork," one officer said.

"Was he trying to take my son?" Michelle's voice wavered, and tears sprang back into her eyes.

"We're not sure. He was interrupted by the child's teacher before he could attempt anything. Nothing he said to the boy gives us an indication of what his purpose was."

She told them about the calls, the letter, the rat's carcass. They asked her a litany of questions. Did Lucius know people in Maryland? In D.C.? When had she last seen him?

"What can be done?" Michelle asked.

One of the officers sighed. Once they had confirmed the court order, a warrant could be issued for Lucius's arrest. They would send extra cars to patrol the school area and her neighborhood. They would also contact the Charleston Police Department so that Lucius would be detained if he returned home.

In the D.C. area, however, they had no known contact for him. They had already checked his credit cards—no trail. Without knowing where to look for him, increasing the patrol around her was all that could be done. This man was smart, they said. He was covering his tracks.

"Should I take Andre out of school? Should I move away?"

They couldn't tell her this but gave her the number for another detective and a victim-witness advocate.

"Just keep a close eye on him," one said. "If your ex-husband shows up again, call us so that we can apprehend him. Don't try to confront him on your own."

Michelle lifted her hand to take the business card the officer was giving her and realized that her hand was shaking. After more questions and more cautions, she calmed herself, collected Andre and took him home.

She had plans for the night, but her plans were changing.

Her first impulse was to try to get away. But she couldn't move again, not unless she was willing to ask Nigel for money. And it might come to that. On her own, it would be impossible to reestablish herself, even if she spent all the money she'd managed to save in Andre's college fund.

And the more she thought about it, the more convinced she was that she couldn't keep seeing Rashad. She couldn't leave Andre alone for any length of time that she didn't have to, and she couldn't embroil Rashad in this mess that Lucius was creating. Even if Lucius was detained, he wouldn't be put away for long, and knowing about Rashad—if he didn't already—would only make Lucius more spiteful and vindictive.

She didn't even want to tell Rashad about all this baby-daddy business.

Knowing how sweet Rashad was, he would probably want to protect them, but how could he? He couldn't be with both of them all the time. It would be a problem for him, and, even worse, it would make her dependent on a man again. She didn't want that, not even if he was a good man for a change.

Lucius was doing just what he'd probably set out to do; he was ruining her life, sucking the happiness right out of it. If Lucius stole Andre from her, what would she do? He wasn't equipped to raise, much less love, a child, but he might do it just to spite her. She never thought for one minute that maybe Lucius wanted to see his son; he had never paid Andre any mind when he'd had the chance. But he owned his own construction company in South Carolina, so he had the means to go someplace where she might never find her son.

Michelle thought of Rashad. She felt herself shutting down, but she didn't know what else to do. She should deal with this on her own first, before bringing someone else into the situation, into her life.

Michelle realized there were three reasons she should keep her plans for the night. Andre would be staying with Nigel and Regina's sitter in an alarmed house, so he would be safe. Her date with Rashad was to go to an art show that included Regina's work, and Michelle wanted to support Regina after all that Regina had done for her. And she needed to find a way to tell Rashad that she couldn't see him anymore.

The last thought made her choke back a sob. She was swallowing her tears so that Andre wouldn't see them.

She was at the dining table with her school books and papers spread out in front of her, but she couldn't focus on them. Andre was in the living room watching *Finding Nemo,* which he'd seen at least three times since they'd visited the National Aquarium—three times in as many days.

She roused Andre from the film, took him to his room to pack his knapsack and then let him go back to the movie while she dressed. It was a special occasion for Regina, so she wanted something nice, but she didn't feel like dressing up, not when it felt like her world was breaking apart.

She put on a red velour riding skirt and a black, crochet hankie-hem top, which she paired with her black boots and a long black cable-knit sweater. She finished it with red earrings, some lipstick and some rouge. Her hair was down, and she added a black headband to it. It seemed to be the right color for the day—the color of mourning.

After she left Andre at Nigel and Regina's, she met Rashad at his house. They were going to take his car to a gallery in downtown D.C. Michelle didn't say anything right away. She needed to get through the night first.

"Hey, beautiful," he said and kissed her.

She thought it would be a brief greeting, but he pulled her in for a long, tender perusal. She shouldn't have let herself, but she got lost in the embrace. With his lips to hers, he drew her into his foyer and let his hands begin to run over her body inside her heavy sweater. When she felt his hands on her breasts, she murmured, feeling herself begin to throb at her center. She felt his hand slip under her skirt and trail up her thighs, and she wanted nothing more than the sweet pressure of his fingers against her sex. A soft moan escaped her, and she felt her hips coming forward. She didn't want to be away from this man.

"I can't wait to make love to you tonight," he said.

His low, masculine voice in her ear sent a ripple through her breasts.

He stepped back and exhaled. "And if we keep doing this, we won't be going anywhere."

Michelle looked into Rashad's face—his full lips, his taut jaw, his sparkling eyes. She wanted to get lost in that rugged landscape.

She refocused her attention. She had to let him go tonight. What was she doing?

What could she do? She could figure out how to take care of business so that it might not be a permanent break. But who knew how long it would take to get Lucius out of her life for good?

"I have something to tell you later on," she said.

He smiled, kissed her nose and wrinkled his brow inquisitively.

"Give me a hint."

"Later, after the show. This is Regina's night, and we better be going."

"I can't wait to meet your family and thank your cousin for helping to bring you here."

They got in Rashad's car, and he turned to her.

"And Thanksgiving."

Thanksgiving. Michelle hadn't even thought about it. It was almost here. She had been asked to spend it with Nigel and Regina, and she was supposed to bring her homemade macaroni and cheese. How was she going to get through that?

"I know I'm late asking, but I hope you'll spend it with my family. They've insisted on seeing you again, and Andre will have a blast with my nieces and nephews. It's at my par—"

"I've already planned to spend Thanksgiving with Nigel and Regina."

"Cancel. Or we can house hop. We can do their place for lunch and drive up to Baltimore in time for leftovers."

"I have work to do for school. Next week is the last week of classes and then come finals."

He touched her face, making her inhale sharply.

"I know. You have a lot on your plate, but we can work something out. Think about it."

The night at the showing went well. Regina's mosaic pieces sold more than the work of any of the other artists. Michelle could look at them and see why.

Rashad got on well with both Regina and Nigel. Regina gave her a thumbs-up sign behind his back to indicate her approval, and Michelle could barely tear him away from the conversations he got into with Nigel—something about old-school music and something about finances and something about Rashad opening his own graphic design firm. The two got on as if they were old friends, and they actually looked like they could be brothers in their matching blue suits.

It only made what she had to do all the harder.

At the end of the night, she and Rashad went back to his home.

She was quiet along the way.

"Tell me what you're thinking," he asked.

She looked down and shook her head, not wanting to start what she had to say in the car.

"We do have to talk," he said. "You need to tell me what's been going on with you."

"What do you mean?"

"You get distant sometimes, distracted. I think something's wrong."

"I have a lot on my plate."

"I know."

He let it go until they got inside. He kissed her before they sat down on his couch, and he wrapped his arm around her loosely on the sofa so that they could face one another as they talked.

But Michelle didn't want to face him. Those gentle brown eyes and full, soft lips made what she had to say too hard. She looked down at her lap, where her fingers played nervously against one another. She knew now that she had started to love this man, but she also knew that she couldn't pull him into the black hole that had taken over her life.

"Rashad, I think we need to take a break."

"What? Are you breaking up with me?"

"I just need some time."

"Time for what? What's going on?"

Time to make sure that my ex-husband doesn't steal my son, she thought. But she didn't say that. She sighed heavily, thinking about all the things she had planned for her life.

"I just have too much going on. Classes ending, finals and final projects coming up, work, my son—it's all too much. I can't spend time with you and do all of that and keep my eye on Andre and give him all of the attention that he deserves."

"Maybe we can give Andre attention together."

Michelle found that her heart was being moved and ruptured at the same time.

"Maybe I can help lighten your load a bit so that we do have time to be together sometimes. I can cook dinner some days or take Andre so that you can study or—"

"With all that I have going on, I can't let Andre become attached to you. He met you once and just adores you. He keeps watching *Finding Nemo* and asking—"

"Doesn't his mother adore me, too?" Rashad asked quietly.

Michelle squirmed under his close scrutiny and couldn't lie.

"That's not the point. I just have too much going on. I need a break."

"What's been going on? Tell me. What's really been bothering you?"

Michelle thought of rushing to her son's preschool that morning and of all the history needed to make someone understand what had led to that point. There was no short answer. No, she didn't want to drag Rashad into this with her. He couldn't right the past or fix the present. He couldn't quit his job and become their bodyguard.

"I just told you what you need to know," she said firmly. "There's too much going on in my life." She stood to go. "There's no use talking more. I'm going to go."

Michelle walked out of Rashad's house without giving him the chance to say more. She picked up Andre from Regina's sitter, and she brought him home.

She spent that night and the next several days trying

not to second-guess herself, but it didn't work. She already missed the possibility of someone in her life. She already missed Rashad.

She made it through Thanksgiving with a brave smile on her face. She didn't tell Regina and Nigel about her breakup with Rashad. She didn't want to answer the kinds of questions they might ask.

She didn't stop second-guessing herself until that weekend, when something happened that let her know without a doubt that Lucius was not simply going to leave her alone to get on with her life and that he would do his best to drag down her and anybody associated with her.

It was partly her own fault. It was Sunday evening, and she had taken Andre with her to go get groceries. When she returned home, she got all the bags to the front door before opening it, but she couldn't get them inside with her new alarm on. She turned it off to move the bags inside and started emptying the hallway. She placed the last two bags on the dining room table and turned from Andre to shut the door and rearm the alarm.

There in the doorway stood Lucius, his large figure filling the frame.

He had a hand on the doorjamb and one foot casually crossed over the other, and he stood watching her with bloodshot eyes and a twisted smirk on his lips. He had a look of hate on his face. She could tell from the redness of his eyes that he had been drinking, and she could tell from the firmness of his stance that he was not yet fully drunk.

He swaggered into the living room as if it were his.

"Come here, son," he said to Andre.

Andre got down off his chair and started to obey.

"Stay right there, Andre," Michelle said.

She had been looking at the central controller for her alarm system. The keypad was near the door, and she lunged across the room to get to it and sound the panic alarm. Lucius was nearer to the door than she was and intercepted her. He grabbed her arms and pushed her back into the room, knocking her down to the floor. Then he started laughing at her.

Andre started to cry and came running to her. He was too small to help her up, but he was trying. He turned to his father and said "no" in the midst of his tears.

Michelle scrambled to her feet in time to see Lucius take a menacing step toward his own son. She moved Andre behind her, getting in front of him, between him and Lucius, and backing them away.

Andre clung to the backs of her legs, his arms circling one of her thighs around the slacks she was wearing. His cries turned into low whimpers.

Lucius took a step toward her.

"You think I won't hit you?"

He raised one of his hands to strike her. Michelle involuntarily cringed, and she heard Andre's cry go up again. She took an impulsive step backward, moving Andre with her.

He'd done it before—hit her. She knew what he was capable of, especially when he'd been drinking. But he had never hit Andre. He knew by instinct where she drew the line, and she was damned if she was going to let him do that.

You won't touch my child, she thought.

"Leave us alone," she said, but her voice cracked. "Leave," she added, but it sounded more like a plea than a command.

Still, Lucius didn't like it.

"Leave." He stepped toward her, forcing her to step back again. "You don't tell me when to leave. Didn't you get my messages? You don't tell me what to do. I pay for you. I'll do what I want to do with you."

He smacked his fist into his palm right in front of her face, forcing her back farther.

"You got my present? That's you, a filthy rat. A whore. You think I don't know about this man you got up here? You tell him he better keep away from my property, or he'll see what he gets. You tell him I pay for you, and I do what I want with you."

"I'm not seeing anyone anymore," she said, worried that Lucius might try to do something to Rashad. She was aware of the irony of it all. "And you're the one who was always chasing after women, all through—"

He smacked his fist into his palm again, and she backed into the wall behind her with Andre wedged between the wall and her legs.

"That's because you can't satisfy a man. And I'll have you whenever I want. I pay for you."

"Don't talk this way in front of a child. You think you're fit to see him? You're not."

Lucius lowered his face to hers and banged his fists against the wall on both sides of her head.

"Hear that? That's what you're going to get soon."

She turned her face from his sour breath but was trapped against the wall and didn't know what else to do.

"Why are you doing this in front of your son? He's four. Four."

"I pay for him, too. You can't keep him from me."

A feeling of panic started to rise inside Michelle. If Lucius tried to take Andre, what could she do?

"You don't have him because you came drunk to the custody hearing and acted a fool. And you won't get my son." It was a strong statement, but with Lucius so close to her face, Michelle found herself speaking just above a whisper.

"You think you got a mouth on you, but I'm making plans for you. See?"

Lucius opened the leather bomber jacket he was wearing, and Michelle could see the handle of a small gun sticking up from the top of his jeans. She gasped.

A siren went by outside, and Lucius took a step back and listened. Michelle could tell that it was a fire engine, but perhaps Lucius was too tipsy to tell the difference between that and the police. In seconds it passed them, fading into the growing darkness.

"I'll come for him when I'm ready."

He backed up and turned toward the open door. He listened momentarily for sounds and then stepped into the hall.

"You're not done with me until I'm done with you," Lucius said.

Michelle kneeled down to take Andre into her arms and her legs buckled beneath her, sinking her to the floor as the sobs started shaking her shoulders.

She heard Lucius yelling outside about her being a whore.

She had only a second to indulge her tears. If the police were going to get him, she needed to call at once. She took a breath, lifted Andre and herself, found the phone on the counter and dialed 911 to report that her ex-husband had entered her apartment and threatened her and had a gun.

"He's still outside." She heard a car start. "Wait, I hear a car starting," she said though her tears. "That could be him, but it's too dark to see anything from up here."

"Try to stay calm, Ms. Johns. A patrol car is in your area."

When she had finished the report, she hung up the phone and sank back down onto the floor with Andre in her arms; his little body shook as he hiccupped sobs. With Lucius gone, the tension that had built up inside Michelle broke through, and her sobs joined Andre's. She pressed him to her chest, scared of losing him.

She had wanted to handle this on her own. Now she felt alone in her turmoil. She held Andre against her and cried, and she couldn't help wishing that Rashad's arms were around her.

Chapter 12

Rashad had spent Thanksgiving with his family in Baltimore, avoiding inquiries about Michelle and tolerating ribbing about her from his brothers.

Now he was on his way to her place to get some answers to inquiries of his own. He refused to let it be over without a real explanation and knew that she hadn't told him the full story. He had to know if she had a viable reason for ending their relationship.

It didn't make sense to him that she was willing to let him go after all that they had shared. What little he did know was leading him to her place for the truth. What little he did know didn't prepare him for what he found when he got there.

When he arrived, her door was open.

"Michelle?" he called, stepping inside.

That's when he heard Andre's sniffles.

"Andre?" he called and rounded the couch.

The path toward the bedrooms was between the couch

and the counter that separated the dining room and the living room. On the floor in front of the counter, he found Michelle holding Andre to her chest and rocking back and forth. There were tears running down her face, and Andre was crying, as well.

Rashad sprinted over to them and knelt down, wrapping his arms around them.

"Michelle, what's happened? Are you all right?"

She pulled Andre closer to her and continued rocking. She nodded and then buried her face against the crown of Andre's head.

"What happened?"

She shook her head and didn't answer.

"Do I need to call the police?"

She shook her head again.

"An ambulance?"

"No."

Rashad moved his arm beneath her knees, lifted them both and carried them to the couch. She seemed in no position to talk, so he kept an arm around her and started rubbing her hair and patting Andre as their tears began to subside.

When he heard the police siren outside, he knew that it was coming there, and he watched the open front door until a blue uniform darkened the frame.

"Michelle Johns?" an officer asked.

Michelle nodded, wiped at the streaks on her face and began to pull herself together to talk to the officers.

"We're aware of your case," said the officer. "Tell us what happened."

"I was bringing in the groceries." She pointed behind her to the bags on the table. "So the alarm was off. My ex-husband, Lucius Vaughn, came in after me."

Rashad listened while Michelle described the events.

He didn't know what had happened already in her "case," but he got a clear picture of that evening.

While one of the officers got on the phone to call in some information, the other asked her more questions. Was this the first time she'd seen Lucius since the other incidents? Did he ever own a gun during their marriage? Could she tell what type of gun it was? Did she see the car? Did she have a recent photograph? What was he wearing?

The officer turned to Rashad. "What about you? Did you see a car leaving the lot on your way in?"

Rashad had to think back. "No, no. But I must have just missed him."

The other officer returned from the phone.

"There's a warrant already out for his arrest from the prior incident, but the gun escalates the case. We're going to canvass the neighborhood for anyone who might have seen the car he was driving and call the Charleston police to see if his registered vehicle is at his house. We've issued another all-points bulletin, and we're increasing patrol of the area."

"What should I do now?"

"Let us handle this, Ms. Johns. We're looking for him now, and we're running his credit cards again. If we're lucky, we'll pick him up before he can leave the state. If not, they'll get him in Charleston when he returns to his known address."

The officers seemed competent and sympathetic. But there also didn't seem to be a great deal they could do. Michelle's ex-husband could be miles away by now, and no one even knew what kind of car he was driving. Rashad was frustrated. He could only imagine what Michelle had been going through, and he wondered for how long.

Rashad was quiet through all of it. Now was not the time for his questions. He gathered some of what had been going on from what was being said and postponed his query.

When the police had gone and the door was closed with the alarm rearmed, Michelle leaned forward, leaving the circle of his arm, and stood. It wasn't late, but Andre was tuckered out from the events of the night, and she carried him to his room. Rashad stood at the door as she pulled back his comforter, laid him down and covered him.

Now that the police were gone, she was silent and she seemed tired.

He waited while she sent an email, and he could see that it was to an attorney, but he didn't pry further. He knew that the hour of revelation was coming.

After she turned off the computer, she went into the dining room to start unpacking the grocery bags. He followed her and began unloading the bags and handing her the groceries, checking the meat and produce and dairy items in case anything had spoiled in the hours they'd been sitting out.

When they were done, he stepped toward her and tried to take her in his arms, but she put her hands up and shook her head.

"Hey," Rashad said. "It's me, the one who cares about you."

He cupped the side of her face and drew her eyes to his. He tugged her toward him and took her in his arms. At first she just accepted his arms around her, but then she put her hands on his chest and laid her head on his shoulder, letting him caress her back and arms and soothe some of the tension out of her.

"Hey," he said after a little while. "It's time for us to talk."

Michelle led the way to the living room, and they sat down on the couch. Michelle pulled her legs up underneath her, and Rashad gave her a little room but stayed close enough to have one arm on the back of the sofa behind her. His other hand was free, and he used it to cover the fingers she had entwined on her lap.

"Tell me what's been going on."

"I don't even know where to start."

"Has this been going on ever since the divorce?"

"It did periodically when I was still in Charleston. That's one of the reasons I moved up here to start over. Then it stopped. My number is unlisted. I don't put return addresses on anything going home. I thought I was in the clear. Then a few weeks ago I got a call. Then an unsigned letter. Then more calls. Then a dead rat on my dining room table. Then he went to Andre's preschool. That was last week, the day of Regina's art show. Now this. I've emailed my lawyer. I've called the police. I've gotten an alarm. I'm not sure what else to do."

"Let the police do their job."

"He never had a gun before."

"They'll find him. Don't worry."

Rashad could tell that his attempts to console her weren't working. He wanted more information.

"Tell me how it got to this point. How did it start? What was your marriage like?"

"You know I married right out of high school. I was eighteen, and back then I went for the bad boys. Lucius was everything I thought I wanted—a rebel, a loner, a fighter, a partier. Things seemed good at first."

"And then?"

"Then came the cheating and the drinking and—"

"Did he hit you?"

"A few times, when he was drunk. It was more verbal abuse—denigration and threatening. That's if he was home and paying attention at all. There was a lot of neglect, especially after Andre came along. He didn't really pay attention to Andre at all, which is why all this is ironic.

He says I can't keep his son from him, but he didn't want Andre when he had him."

"He's just using Andre to threaten you."

"Well, he knows how to push my buttons because that'll do it. What if he took Andre? What if I couldn't find them?"

"Does he have the means to do something like that?"

"He owns a construction company, and he's good at construction. If he sold his company… Who knows? I had Andre when I was twenty-one, after three years of marriage. We were divorced when I was twenty-three and Andre was two."

"And that was over two years ago?"

"Yeah, we've been in the D.C. area for just over two and a half years. I wanted to get away from Lucius, get back to school, start a new life. I wanted to put all that behind me—the ugly divorce, being wild, being… It was like being in a prison, never knowing when the siren would sound, never knowing when he'd be there, when he'd be gone, when he'd be drunk, when he'd be in a good mood—which could be just as bad."

Rashad didn't know the man, only that he didn't like him. He was angry over what this man had done to Michelle, to Andre. But he knew it was best to appear calm.

"You said the divorce was ugly. What happened? You got custody. You got to leave the state."

"I got sole custody because he showed up to the court hearing drunk and belligerent. The divorce proceeding—he lied through the whole thing and told every reckless thing I'd ever done. He didn't want to pay alimony or child support. But we were able to catch him in so many lies that he lost all credibility. He was furious. That's when that taunting and harassing started. I had to get a restraining order against him. He's buddies with half the police force in our area. It did nothing. But there were a couple of arrests, and when I petitioned to leave, it was granted." Michelle shook her head. "I thought it would end. But here it is."

"You said it seemed good at first."

"Yeah."

"But he never pleased you sexually."

"He was just…all about him. But then so was every other guy I'd known. That or they just didn't know what to do. And neither did I. He disparaged me about that, too. But it didn't stop him." She shook her head. "What a mess. My whole marriage was a mess."

Rashad wanted to know more, but he didn't want to push. What she'd said already explained a lot—why she seemed so grateful for kindness, why she worked so hard, why she hadn't dated in over two years, why she didn't seem to believe that he wanted to hang out with her son, why she'd been getting more and more skittish and distracted.

"Now you see," she said, "why we shouldn't see each other right now. I have too much going on, and I need to deal with this."

"No, I don't see," he answered. "And you don't have to deal with it alone."

"My being with someone just seems to rile him more, give him more ammunition for his rants and threats."

"You being alone just lets him win in whatever game he's playing—a game where the goal is to intimidate you."

"Well, he is winning, isn't he? What's going to happen? The police pick him up here or down home. He does a little time. It starts over. How can I win?"

"To start, you win by having your own life. You win by doing what you're already doing, which is getting on with your life. Which I hope includes me."

Rashad started to rub Michelle's fingers, but she stopped him. She shook her head.

"I don't want to put you in danger."

"Then let me help keep you and Andre out of danger. Let me help look out for both of you."

Rashad moved the arm he had around her and cupped the nape of Michelle's neck. He began massaging her neck and was rewarded when she stretched her head to each side and let it fall back into his hand.

"Why didn't you tell me all of this before? Don't you know I have feelings for you?" he asked.

"I didn't want to get you embroiled in all this ex-husband, baby-daddy drama," she said. "It would turn anybody off."

"Not me."

"But what can you do? You can't be with us all the time."

"For one, you're not staying here for a while. And he might know to look for you at your cousin's. If you won't stay with me, I'll put you up in a hotel. Come stay with me for a little while. Let's figure this out together."

Michelle still hesitated.

"I would feel better seeing that you're both safe."

"Okay. We can stay with you for a few days."

"Good."

Rashad drew Michelle toward him and into a hug.

They rose, bagged the perishables in the fridge and put all the meat in the freezer except for a package of ground meat; Rashad was making them spaghetti for dinner at his place. Michelle woke up Andre and packed small suitcases for them both, and then she followed Rashad to his house.

Rashad let them in, and Shaka took turns jumping on Michelle and Andre until Rashad closed him in his bedroom so that he could get dinner going. Michelle and Andre were taking his guest room, and he stowed their bags before dinner. Rashad couldn't help but wish that Michelle's things were going in another room—his. After tonight he had a lot of new information to digest, but there was one thing he knew. Regardless of her ex-husband—and the man was clearly a bit psycho—he still wanted this woman.

Chapter 13

Michelle put the ribs back in the oven and checked the rice.

She had called in to work and taken the week off, and she had informed Mrs. Miller that they would be away for a few days. She and Andre were still going to school; she didn't want him to miss anything, and this was the last week of classes at Howard, so she couldn't afford to miss them. Other than that, they would be staying inside as much as possible.

She had picked up Andre as his class let out and brought him back to Rashad's house. Now she stood in Rashad's kitchen, looking for some parsley in his seasoning cabinet. The least she could do was cook.

Andre was sitting at Rashad's massive dining table tracing his letters, and Shaka was wandering back and forth between the two of them, circling their legs.

Suddenly, Shaka let out a yelp and bounded for the foyer. She heard Rashad's voice.

"They let you out, Shaka? You're my big boy." Then he put on his deep voice. "Manly Shaka."

Michelle couldn't help laughing.

She saw Rashad pat Andre on the head on his way into the kitchen, where he kissed her briefly, laid his satchel on the counter and let Shaka out into the backyard.

"You can leave him in my room. He won't mind—after a while, at least," he said.

"He's no problem. Andre loves him."

"Did you get in touch with your lawyer today?"

"Yes, I emailed her, and she called me back. She checked to see that the police down there were being kept up on the warrants issued up here and made sure that the police up here had copies of the restraining orders filed down there. That's all she can do."

Michelle sighed heavily, and Rashad came to her and rubbed her upper arms.

"I also called the detective, the one whose number I was given after Lucius went to Andre's school. I'm going to meet with him tomorrow before I pick up Andre."

"What time?"

"At one o'clock," Michelle said.

"I'm coming. I'll meet you here," Rashad insisted.

"You don't have to—"

"I want to," he said. "I smell something good."

Michelle smiled. She was happy to have done something for Rashad in return for all that he was doing for her.

"I stopped at the grocery store after I picked up Andre. The ribs are almost done, and if I can find a frying pan, the vegetables will be the last thing."

Rashad smiled and kissed her nose and then pulled a frying pan down from the upper cabinet.

"Now if the pots are at the bottom," Michelle said, "why are the frying pans in the upper cabinets?"

"I do that deliberately so as to confuse my houseguests."

Rashad laughed. “No, I plan to get one of those racks and hang all the pots up so you can see them.”

“Uh-huh.” Michelle smiled again. “You need help.”

“Can I do anything?”

“No, relax.”

Rashad went into the dining room and sat next to Andre while Michelle sautéed the vegetables. Soon she heard Rashad giving Andre tips on writing his letters. Then Rashad asked Andre about some game. After they had dinner together, they sat in front of the computer, and Rashad showed Andre how to play the game he’d asked about earlier. The two seemed to have fun, and Michelle was grateful for Rashad’s attention to Andre.

“Can you play alone now, Andre?” Michelle asked.

Andre nodded.

“I can watch him,” she said to Rashad. “You can change and rest or do what you usually do. You don’t have to entertain us.”

“I usually think about you,” he said softly. Then he turned his attention back to Andre. “Besides, it’s time for Perfection!”

“What’s that?” Andre asked.

“It’s a game I play with my nieces and nephews. You set a timer. Then you have to match the shapes to the slots they go in before they all pop up. You game?” he asked Andre.

“Can I play, Mommy?”

“If Mom says yes, we can all play.”

They played for over an hour, laughing when the adults, who got less time on the timer, couldn’t beat a four-year-old.

Michelle put Andre in their bed and decided to turn in early herself, though she sat up next to him for a while reading some of her homework, ever aware that Rashad was right in the next room.

The next day he met her at his home at noon, and they

drove to Greenbelt to see the detective. He'd been kept up on her case and assured her that they were looking for Lucius. They had an all-points bulletin out, and Lucius's photograph had been distributed to all their officers. They continued to check his credit cards, and had started checking for car rentals, as his own licensed vehicle was still in his drive. They also had Charleston police interviewing family members for information on any other known acquaintances in the D.C. area. They were doing all that could be done. She needed to be patient.

This was not really what Michelle wanted to hear, but at least they were doing what they could.

"What if you find him?" she asked. "How long will he be in jail for this?"

"That's hard to say. Violating a restraining order. Harassment. Armed assault. Possibly an unregistered weapon."

"We'll ask your lawyer," Rashad said to her.

"That's a good idea," the detective said.

Michelle shook her head. They could find out how long, but whatever it was, it wouldn't be forever. And then this would start again. Nothing would really end it.

Michelle thought this, but she didn't say it. She didn't want Rashad to try to console her when there was simply no consolation to be had. She listened as the detective reminded her to be aware of her surroundings, to keep a vigilant eye on Andre, to call them the moment Lucius reappeared and to avoid trying to handle him herself.

He gave her the number again for the victim-witness advocate and let her call to make an appointment. She got one for that Friday, and then she and Rashad went to pick up Andre.

They had arranged to have dinner at Nigel and Regina's that night so that Michelle could tell them what was going on. She didn't want to say much, but she had to at least make them aware that Lucius was about and was armed and might look for her there.

"Why didn't you come to us before?" Nigel asked.

Rashad was nodding, and she elbowed him gently for taking sides.

"You know we're here for you," Regina echoed. "Maybe you should move in with us. We have an alarm system."

"So do I," Michelle said. "And I won't make the mistake of disarming it again, not for a minute."

"Who from home knew your number here besides us?" Nigel asked.

"My mother and father, my lawyer," she answered. "I think that's it."

"You need to talk to your mother," Nigel said. "See if she gave your number to anyone."

Michelle hadn't thought of that. She hadn't wanted to worry her folks, but who else had her number, and how else could Lucius have gotten it?

"You know, I need to do that. I'll check on Andre and give my mom a call."

While Rashad, Nigel and Regina continued to talk at the dining table, with Sharon asleep in her bassinet near Regina, Michelle went into the living to check on Andre, who was watching television. Then she slipped upstairs to the den to make her call.

"Hello."

"Hey, Mom."

"How's my girl? How's my grandson?"

"We're fine, Mom. But we need to talk."

"Why, honey? What's wrong?"

Michelle had to figure out how to find out what she needed to know without giving too much information.

"Mom, do you have any idea how Lucius got my home number? Have you given it to anyone?"

"Did he call you, honey? He probably just realizes what

he's missing and wants you back. Don't you pay him any mind. His mother says he's not doing so well. With the economy being what it is, his construction business isn't taking in what it used to."

"You've been talking to Mrs. Vaughn?"

"She tells me that without his wife and son to keep him at least somewhat stable, Lucius has been getting himself into all kinds of trouble. He's been drinking more and has had fights in bars."

Michelle knew this pattern well. The more things spiraled out of control, the more aggressive Lucius became and the more he partied and drank. The more he drank, the more desperate and aggressive he became and the more things spiraled out of control. When things picked up, he would level out. He would come home more; he would be less evil spirited with his men at work. He didn't care about her then, either, but he was less of a terror.

"He probably wants what he didn't know he had," her mother said. "See how things come around?"

If his business wasn't doing well, he would be even angrier about having to pay alimony and child support. Maybe if she could make it on her own, he would leave her alone. But none of this answered her question.

"Mom, did you give anyone my number? Did you give it to Mrs. Vaughn?"

"She just wanted to speak with her grandbaby, honey. She said she wouldn't tell it to a living soul. Hasn't she called you yet?"

"She hasn't, but he has. Mom, we agreed that no one could have that number."

Once Lucius got the number and figured out what area she was in, he could have done some kind of online search to get her address, or he could have figured she'd be in touch with Nigel and kept tabs on him.

"He just wants you in his pocket. But don't worry, honey. That's not going to happen."

Michelle hung up without giving her mother any additional details. She was more despondent than when she'd started.

Back downstairs, she took her seat next to Rashad, who put his arm around her.

"You were right, Nigel. My mother gave my number to his mother so she could speak to her grandchild, and here we are."

"I hope they find him soon," Regina said.

And then what? Michelle thought. It would be a brief reprieve at best.

"They will," Rashad said and rubbed her shoulders. "Don't look so worried."

Michelle tried to smile.

"I'm sorry to drag you all into this," she said. Then she looked at Nigel and Regina. "I just wanted you to know that he was about and might look here."

"How long are you staying with Rashad?"

"Until they find him," Rashad said.

"A few days," Michelle said.

"We're more than willing to have you here," Regina reiterated.

Regina got up and began clearing the dishes. Michelle got up to help.

"I'll be okay at home. But thanks."

When they left Nigel and Regina's, it was late. Andre slept on the way to Rashad's house, and Michelle put him to bed once they got inside.

She and Rashad stayed up for a little while. She had a final paper to finish, and he had to catch up on some things he hadn't gotten done at work. Michelle was comfortable sharing his little den with him. She felt safe there, and she liked being in Rashad's space. And just watching him when he was giving Andre attention let her know what she'd been missing during her marriage.

After Rashad kissed her good-night, Michelle checked on Andre and got in the bathtub off the guest bedroom to take a real bath for a change.

Being there with Rashad felt like being on vacation, but she knew her "vacation" had to end soon. She didn't want to stay until Rashad started to miss his own space and his own life. She loved being there, but she didn't want to become a bother.

The next day, she got Andre to school, came back to do some studying, got to class, picked up Andre and got dinner on the stove. She could get used to this.

While she started on the dishes, Rashad found something on television for Andre and Shaka to watch and then came to help her. When she was on the last dish, he moved behind her and encircled her in his arms, kissing her neck. He moved a hand to her breast, and her whole body responded to his touch, her hips pressing back against his. He hummed in her ear, and the low, masculine sound sent ripples down her back and into her groin. Yes, she could really get used to this.

He released her and smiled. She leaned up and kissed him briefly. Then he wrapped his arm around her, and they went into the living room.

"Round two of Perfection," he announced.

"Yeah," Andre agreed.

Shaka yelped, as well.

When Andre started to get tired, Michelle watched as Rashad lifted her son to his shoulder and rocked him. She followed as Rashad brought Andre to their bedroom. Rashad made a game of changing Andre's clothes and asked him if he had brought a book of bedtime stories.

She and Rashad took turns reading and making funny voices for the characters until Andre drifted off.

Before he left her, Rashad looked at her with such passion in his eyes that it made her hold her breath. Then he told her where he would be if she needed him and kissed her gently before leaving her room. She could definitely get used to this.

Michelle stared after him. This man was moving her heart.

Chapter 14

Rashad went into his den but left the door ajar in case Michelle or Andre needed him. Shaka followed him in and curled up on his doggy bed in the corner.

Rashad was still chuckling from reading the story to Andre with Michelle. They'd put on corny voices for the characters and probably had had more fun doing it than groggy little Andre had had listening.

He loved having them all up in his space, and he wished that Michelle were with him then—alone in this room. He'd been wanting her more and more, and tonight he was dying to make love to her. He knew to put on the brakes with Andre there, but that didn't stop him from dreaming.

And he wouldn't trade having Andre there for anything. Rashad often played with his nieces and nephews, but this was his first real indication of what it would be like to raise a child, and he liked taking care of Andre. In fact, it was his first real indication of what it would be like to be with Michelle and Andre full-time, and he liked taking care of them both.

He caught up on some work and got ahead a little because the next afternoon he had taken off so that they could go see his brother Marcus. Michelle had a lawyer in Charleston. She needed someone in the D.C. area, too.

When they got there, Marcus was already expecting them. They planned for a meeting at Marcus's firm and then lunch together at a restaurant downtown. Marcus hugged them both when they came in, and he winked at his baby brother on the sly.

Marcus was the second oldest of the four brothers and was the peacemaker of the bunch. He generally agreed with Derrick (the eldest) but was perhaps more diplomatic in his expression because he was less judgmental. Today he was handling something for his baby brother, so though he was warm and genial, he was also serious and attentive. He took off his navy blazer and leaned forward against his large walnut desk. He motioned Rashad and Michelle into two of the brown leather chairs facing the desk, and then they sat down to the business at hand.

Michelle started to give a summary of what had been happening. Marcus stopped her and called in one of his colleagues who had done more work with her type of case; then he told her to start over.

When Michelle was finished, the other lawyer ran off a checklist of things that her lawyer should do.

"My lawyer's done all of that," Michelle said. "I need to know what else I can do. I need to know whether I need a lawyer here. I need to know how much time he'll get when he's finally arrested."

"The amount of time differs by state and according to what he gets convicted for. Our best bet in this case would be aggravated assault with a dangerous weapon, which has a maximum sentence of ten years in D.C. That means he could get anywhere up to ten years. Ten years is not automatic," the lawyer clarified.

Michelle nodded in understanding.

"You don't need a lawyer in D.C. right now. Your lawyer at home seems to have things covered. When he's arrested and a trial comes up, I can consult with your lawyer, if needed, regarding D.C. statutes. In terms of what you can do, I can refer you to a victim-witness advocate."

"I already have an appointment to see one tomorrow," Michelle said.

"Then you're covering all the bases. Why don't you come to my office with me so I can give you some information I have on harassment and assault under D.C. law."

"Yes. Thank you," Michelle said.

"We'll be right back," the lawyer said.

When they had gone, Marcus gave his little brother a stern look.

"What?"

"I didn't say anything."

"Don't start on me today," Rashad said.

"Are you sure you want to get involved with this, baby bro? This is some—"

"Oh. Oh. This from the one who's always chiding me to get serious."

"I'm not telling you what to do," his brother said. "Look, I like her a lot. But I'm also concerned for you. I just want to make sure you're thinking about what you're getting into before—"

Rashad held up his hand. "I'm thinking about it. I'm thinking about it a lot."

Marcus sat back in his chair. "So you're really into this woman."

Rashad smiled and kicked his leg over the arm of the chair across from his brother. "I really am."

"Well, take it slowly. Okay?"

"Too late for that."

"Then just be careful with this ex-husband of hers running around loose out there. He's dangerous. And this isn't play."

"I am. I will."

Marcus looked at Rashad and smiled. "You might finally be growing up."

"See," Rashad said. "Now you're starting." But then he smiled back nevertheless.

When Michelle came back, the three went to lunch. Then Michelle headed on to school, and Rashad went back to work. He'd be staying late to make up for lost time on his current project, and he couldn't wait to get home. Having Michelle and Andre there was like having a family to go home to—a son to play with and teach stuff to, a wife to love. Rashad liked the setup.

He didn't get to play with Andre that night because he got home too late. He was just in time to help put Andre down. Then Michelle dished out a pork chop and some pasta for him and kept him company while he ate. They watched the ten o'clock news on television in the living room downstairs, and both were getting groggy before it was over.

Michelle turned off the news and got up.

"We better get some sleep," she said.

She smiled and reached out her hand to pull him up. But her smile made him really want to play. Instead of getting up to meet her, he pulled her down onto his lap and into his arms. He had been wanting to feel her body against his for a long time, and now that he had her close, his body flamed.

She took hold of his neck and kissed him deeply. Perhaps she had been wanting him, too.

"Thank you for this week," she said quietly.

"Don't thank me. I want to be here for you," he said and then reclaimed her lips.

She had changed into her home clothes before he got there, and she had on a long-sleeved blue T-shirt with a blue sweater and navy leggings. He slipped his hand inside her sweater and found one of her breasts.

She let out a breath and covered his hand with hers, pressing it to her chest as it kneaded her breast into a hard peak. Her mouth opened under his, and her hips tilted on his thighs. Yes, she had definitely been wanting him, too.

He had taken off his tie when he hit the front door. Michelle undid two of his buttons and ran her fingers along his chest, bewitching him. When she found one of his nipples and squeezed it between her fingers, his sex leaped, and he pulled her against the hard bulge building against her hip.

She reached between them and ran her fingers over his crest again. He murmured quietly and stirred beneath her. This woman knew how to turn him on.

Rashad pulled his lips from hers and brought her neck to his mouth, running his tongue along her collarbone before kissing the center of her throat. He moved his hand down from her breast over her stomach to the valley between her legs. He wished she had on a dress so that he could touch her freely; instead, he began to massage her through the knit weave of her leggings. Her head fell back, and her knees drew open to allow his caress. Her eyes fluttered shut, and she sighed heavily.

Her hand still played between them, making him want to pull her into a straddle and ride against her. He repossessed her mouth to stop himself from moaning, and he kneaded her center harder, until her hips were rotating over his lap, driving him to distraction.

They toyed with each other until they were both wet and wanting, both ready for each other, both breathing hard.

When Shaka leaped on her lap, it jolted them both. He made a seat there, wagging his tail.

They both turned to the little terrier, then back to each other.

"We should stop," she said, glancing up the steps.

"I know," he conceded. "I guess it's time for bed."

Rashad scooped his hand under Shaka's belly and lifted him from Michelle's lap. With his other hand, he steadied her as she stood up, still weak with pleasure. He wanted nothing more than to touch her until that pleasure consumed her and then peel off her clothes and start again. He wanted nothing more than to carry her to his room, to his bed, and feel her naked body against his all night. He wanted nothing more than this woman.

Rashad refocused his mind and tried to calm his body. *In time,* he told himself.

He climbed the stairs with her hand in his. He dipped his head into his guest room to check on Andre, who was fast asleep, and left Michelle at the door with a brief kiss. Yes, he liked this setup.

The next morning before going to work Rashad went with Michelle to Greenbelt to see the victim-witness advocate. She told them the same thing that the others had told them, except that she added one additional possibility—one that Rashad didn't like.

"If you need to relocate, either temporarily or permanently, I can provide you with assistance in doing that. I can also help you communicate with the police and the legal system, and I can put you in touch with a variety of agencies that provide services for women in your position. Counseling can be an important part of the recovery process for—"

"What do I do now to protect my son?"

"Short of relocating, you can let the police do their job."

Rashad and Michelle talked about it all the way home.

"What about Andre's schooling? What about my finals? My job?"

"Stay with me," Rashad said. "I love having you there."

"I don't think that's what she meant," Michelle responded.

"Andre can transfer schools. We can—"

"I'll still be in the same general area. All he has to do is follow Nigel or Regina until I go to see them. If he isn't caught—"

"He will be caught. He has to go home sometime. He has to use his credit cards eventually. Hey, he'll probably call to check on his company or to speak to his mother at some point, too. Can we talk to the detective about checking those records?"

"I'll call him when I get home. But…I don't know. I'm tired of having to hide. I'm tired of waiting to have my life back, even my own bed."

"Let's think about this a bit and talk more tonight."

Rashad dropped Michelle off at home, saw that she got inside safely and headed to work. He was disturbed by the thought of her leaving—relocating. But then what would he do if something happened to Andre? Or to her? It seemed perfect that she and Andre stay with him. It made fantastic sense. But he could hear in her tone that she was already itching for her own place—her own bed, as she put it.

They talked more that night, but they didn't reach a conclusion on the idea of relocation. In fact, the only thing that came out as certain was that Michelle would be going home on Sunday night.

"We only brought clothes for a week, and I'm back to work next week. This wasn't supposed to be permanent. We don't want to overstay our welcome," she said and held up her hand to stop him from interrupting. "And if we need to stay somewhere else, we'll stay with Nigel and Regina for a bit."

She wouldn't hear any opposition, so he left it alone—at least for the night.

The next day, Saturday, they slept in a little, had a late breakfast and ran some errands. He needed some groceries, office supplies and a few bulk items, mainly paper supplies. She needed things from the pharmacy, and Andre was along for the ride. After errands, they spent some time working—her on school, him on work and Andre on the computerized tablet that Rashad had given him.

When Andre got restless, Rashad took him out into the backyard with Shaka, and being that there still wasn't any snow yet, they spent the time making progress on a brick barbecue pit installation that Rashad had gotten for his last birthday from his brothers and had never finished. Once they were tired of that, they played fetch with Shaka for a while and then did some rearranging in Rashad's garage. All of this was to give Michelle some quiet time to get her studying done.

Rashad sat down on the back step leading to his kitchen. The concrete was a bit cold, and Andre got up from next to him and came to take a seat on Rashad's knee.

Rashad rubbed Andre's head and circled Andre's waist with his arm. Andre began to swing himself back and forth by rocking Rashad's knee from side to side.

"We're going to have to build you a swing set when it gets warm. Would you like that?"

"Uh-huh. Where will we put it?"

Rashad looked around his yard, which wasn't very large. "Well, with the barbecue pit going in there," he said, pointing to their growing tower of brick, "we'll have to put it over there." He pointed to the other side of the yard. "We'll need a table in between for when we use the barbecue."

"I can have a swing at your house?"

"You most certainly can."

Andre smiled.

"What should we do for dinner?" he asked Andre. "Do you want to fix something with me, or should we take Mommy out to dinner?"

"Out."

"Where would Mommy want to go eat?"

"Jelly Belly," Andre said, his face lighting up.

Rashad laughed. Jelly Belly was a children's restaurant. "Hmm. I think that's where you want to go eat," he said, tickling Andre's tummy through his parka. "I don't know if that's Mommy's favorite place. But I think we can go there."

Shaka wandered over to them, and Andre bent over to pet him. When Shaka wandered back into the yard, Andre turned to him.

"Rashad?"

"What is it?"

"Do you know my daddy, too?" Andre asked.

"No, I don't."

"He's mean to Mommy."

"Is he mean to you sometimes, too?"

Andre nodded slowly.

"That's not nice," Rashad said, wanting to tread carefully. "Daddy is a troubled man. And when you're troubled, sometimes you're mean to the people you should love. We're going to try to get Daddy some help. You and Mommy are going to be okay." He rubbed Andre's head. "Okay?"

Andre nodded again. Rashad gave him a hug, and, without thinking, he kissed Andre's forehead.

"Let's go see if Mommy wants to go to Jelly Belly."

"Okay."

Rashad stood, lifting Andre to his hip as he did. He turned toward the door and whistled for Shaka, who came yelping. Funny, Michelle was worried about Andre getting attached to him. Here he was starting to get attached to Andre.

At dinner, the subject of prolonging their stay with him came up again.

"I want to stay, Mommy," Andre said, joining him.

"We've interrupted Rashad's life enough," she said to Andre. "He's missed work. We have him spending money on groceries. We've taken over his evenings. And we don't know how long this can take. We're out of clean clothes, and we—"

"I'm caught up with work, and I've loved having you with me."

"Can't we stay with Rashad?" Andre asked.

"We're going home tomorrow night," Michelle said. "End of debate."

Andre pouted, but only until they had finished eating, when he got to play on the slides.

For their last night together, they decided to watch a movie and stopped to get a new one on the way home. Andre picked an animated film about wizards and dragons, and the three gathered on the couch with popcorn.

Halfway through, Andre got down, rounded his mother's legs and got up onto Rashad's lap. Rashad left one arm around Michelle and drew the other around Andre's waist. After the film, they turned to a children's channel, and by the time the first show was over, Andre had fallen asleep against his chest.

"I think I tuckered him out this afternoon," Rashad said and chuckled. "We put a few layers on the pit and then straightened out the garage a bit."

"Thank you for watching him."

"You don't have to thank me. I enjoyed it. I enjoy watching over both of you. I wish you would stay."

Michelle shook her head decisively, and the two rose to bring Andre upstairs to bed.

After he was changed and tucked in, Rashad and Michelle moved into the den to do some more studying and work. Rashad wanted to try to reason with her again about staying with him, but he could tell that she wasn't going to change her mind. He understood that she wanted to be in her own space and was tired of hiding and whatever else her reasons were, but he also planned to keep a close eye on her, and he was sure he'd be spending some nights on her couch.

He'd never felt closer to a woman before than he felt to Michelle right then, and despite the fact that she was determined to leave, he could tell that she felt close to him, as well. With Andre there, they hadn't been intimate over the past week, but the intimacy that had sprung up among the three of them had made them feel like a family.

Rashad got in bed late that night, tired from the day. He wished that Michelle was joining him on the California king. Michelle might want her own space back, but Rashad had no intention of letting her go.

Chapter 15

Michelle entered the security code for her alarm on the keypad and turned back into the living room. Rashad had just left after seeing them home and checking out the apartment. Now she needed to get some meat out of the freezer for dinner, get a load of laundry going, get clothes out for the next day and get Andre started on his homework. Her "vacation" was over.

Being at Rashad's place had made her feel safe. His presence was there even when he wasn't. And she loved that presence. Now she was a bit on edge again, but she tried not to let that show for Andre's sake.

She hadn't actually wanted to leave, but she did need to get on with her life, and there was no telling how long it might take before Lucius was caught. She had started getting used to being at Rashad's, and Andre had started getting used to Rashad. She liked that, but she didn't want to force an evolution in their relationship because of her ex-husband's trifling. And she was interrupting his life, his work, his routine. She could see the black hole in her life spreading into his, and that frustrated her.

She also needed to get back to work and to get ready for her finals and to get her final projects done. And she needed to think about moving once the semester was over. She planned to see the victim-witness advocate again before she decided. If that was what she had to do to keep Andre safe, then it would be done. Being with Rashad didn't let her consider that possibility as a real one.

Now that he knew about her past and her trouble with her ex-husband, he seemed just as eager to see her as before, but she still felt guilty for imposing her problems on him. He called every day and came by at least every other evening that first week she was home, and he showed no signs of slacking off.

By the next weekend, they had plans. On Sunday they would take Andre with them to run some errands and do some Christmas shopping. It was already December, and with all that was going on, Michelle hadn't given any thought to the holiday season.

Rashad was on time for their date to do Christmas shopping. He closed her door behind him, and she recoded the alarm. He met her as she turned with a kiss on her lips. The gentle pressure of his lips stopped her in her tracks and sent a flood of warmth through her body. And when Rashad saw the effect that it had on her, a bright smile spread over his face, shading the passion that was in his eyes with victory.

He cocked his head, looking for Andre. Not seeing him, Rashad pulled her against his chest and kissed her again. His thick, soft lips parted hers and his tongue slipped into her mouth.

Michelle felt her breasts graze along his black wool overcoat, and her mouth opened to the warmth of his tongue inside her. She let out an involuntary murmur as another smile covered his face.

He pulled his mouth from hers and moved it to her ear.

"I want you, beautiful," he whispered in her ear.

That time when he kissed her, her arms went around his neck, and her body pressed against his.

"Soon," he said. He let out a breath and took her hand, leading her into her own living room.

"Where's my little rug rat?"

"Getting dressed." She turned toward Andre's room and called out, "Andre, honey, are you almost ready?"

"Yes, Mommy."

"Go to the bathroom and then come get your coat on. Rashad's here."

Andre came bolting from his room and ran to Rashad, who lifted him for a hug and set him down next to her.

The affection Andre had for Rashad stirred her, and Michelle rubbed Andre's head before opening his coat for him.

"Wait," Rashad said, turning to Andre. "Did you go to the bathroom?"

Andre pursed his lips and then headed back to his room.

Michelle and Rashad chuckled.

"Good catch," Michelle said. "Thank you for being so good to Andre," she added.

"Stop thanking me. He's a sweet kid. It's easy to be good to him, as easy as it is to be good to his mother."

Rashad unbuttoned the bottom of his coat, took a seat next to her and wrapped his arm around her. She stopped fighting her temptations and put her hand into his. When he smiled at that, she pulled him toward her by his scarf and kissed his lips. After she pulled back, she set her gaze on Andre's door and slipped her hand between the open buttons at the bottom of his coat. She found his manhood and moved her palm over it until it was pressing against her hand.

Rashad's eyes glazed over with a look of pure passion. He cleared his throat and said, "Very, very soon."

Michelle laughed at his reaction and withdrew her hand before Andre emerged from his room.

Rashad closed his coat, and they stood. She had on a pair of red denim leggings, a red pullover and her black flats, and she went to pull her long black cable-knit sweater out of the front closet.

Rashad was helping Andre into his coat. He looked over at her.

"Do you need a winter coat?" he asked.

"No, I do not," she said emphatically, to end any inkling he might be having of shopping for her. "I have one. It's not cold enough for it yet. And this is a very warm sweater. Hey, if you're thinking of getting me something for Christmas, you can make up for the chocolate fiasco."

They both laughed.

"Actually," she said, "do you have gloves?"

"No, you won't be getting me gloves for Christmas," Rashad said. "I want something far more romantic."

"Hey, whatever you need is romantic," she said. She added, "What do you consider romantic?"

Rashad's eyes lit up and he said, "Ask me later, and I'll definitely tell you."

Rashad had put on Andre's coat. Now he picked up Andre like an airplane and spun him around. After that, he settled her son on his hip, ready to go. Michelle adjusted her sweater and scarf, wrapped a scarf around Andre and entered the security code on her alarm. Then they headed outside.

"What's first?" Rashad asked.

"Groceries are last," Michelle said. "Hey, who's driving this time?"

"Do you know your way to the mall in Wheaton?"

The look she gave him made Rashad start to laugh. She continued to give him this look.

"Okay, okay. You drive, but let's take my car."

Michelle nipped that in the bud by going to her car, ushering Andre into the booster seat in the back, settling him in and opening the door for Rashad.

"Okay," he said. "Let's take your car."

"First stop?" she asked.

"Well, I need a few things at Wheaton."

"Just tell me which way."

At Wheaton Plaza, Rashad had them stop in Kay Jewelers. He was getting his brothers engraved gold ID bracelets like the one he'd gotten for his father. And since gold seemed to be his family theme that year, he had Michelle help him pick out something for his mother. Michelle decided on a gold heart with a flower in the middle; the back of it could be engraved, so it seemed to fit with his theme.

By the end of the day, they had gotten iPods, Kindles or Nooks for all of Rashad's in-laws, and his older nieces and nephews. They had also gotten speech recognition software for his dad and gift cards for all of the other adults on his list. Michelle was a bit daunted by his extravagance. She had gotten only a silver bracelet for her mom, a wallet for her dad, hair things for Regina and Mrs. Miller and cuff links for Nigel.

"I can't wait to give you one of my credit cards," Rashad said to her out of the blue.

"What on earth would make you do that?"

He kissed her briefly and looked at her seriously. "When we're married, you get to spend my money."

Michelle's heart faltered and her breath stopped, but what she said—that is, when she could finally talk—was designed to check such wild fantasies.

"I do all right on my own, actually. I don't think I would need to spend your money, even if we were married."

"Not need to but can. And not if but when."

Michelle shook her head and decided not to enter the fray. She tugged Andre's sleeve to draw him back in the direction they were going.

After the mall, the next stop was a toy store. Rashad needed to get things for the rest of his nieces and nephews, and Michelle needed something for Sharon and to collect options for what to get for Andre.

After Rashad found toys for his younger nieces and nephews, he and Michelle followed Andre around the store, observing what he picked up, what he played with longer and what he asked for. At one point, Rashad turned to her and gave her the double thumbs-up signal.

"Eureka. I know what I'm getting him."

"You don't have to get him anything, Rashad."

He put his hands up. "Don't start."

"Fine. Now help me figure out what to get him."

"Hey, you're on your own."

Michelle swatted at him playfully and continued to follow Andre around the store while Rashad hung back, apparently to get Andre's present.

Before they finished at the toy store, Michelle got Andre a puzzle and a paint set so that he wouldn't have to leave a toy store empty-handed. They had pizza at a little Italian restaurant, and Rashad saw them back inside her apartment before taking off. Michelle reset her alarm with Rashad's kiss still warming her lips.

The next week, Rashad kept up his routine of calling frequently and of visiting often during the evening. Michelle loved having him with them and being in touch with him, but she hated that he had to worry about their safety, as he was clearly doing.

There had been no further sign of Lucius, but he hadn't been apprehended. Michelle kept in touch with the police and her lawyer, and she made an appointment to see the victim-witness advocate again once she made it through her communications law final. Outside of his frequent evening check-ins, she'd be seeing Rashad again the following Saturday, which she had off from work.

Rashad picked them up at noon and started by keeping his promise to take Andre to the National Air and Space Museum, where they spent the afternoon. Rashad had gotten them tickets, and they divided their time between the historic aircraft and the spacecraft, with a 3-D movie in the middle.

Andre loved it as much as the National Aquarium in Baltimore. The museum shop was huge and had three levels, and Rashad got Andre books on aviation and space travel, as well as a model plane that he said they would build together.

The afternoon was all about Andre, but the rest of the day was about them. They dropped Andre off with Nigel and Regina in time for him to have dinner with them; he was also spending the night there. After that, they went to dinner in Adams Morgan, a multicultural hub in D.C. Michelle had never been there before and had a hard time choosing which cuisine to try because there were so many. Rashad suggested French, and they selected a place called La Fourchette.

After that he took her to the National Mall to see the Martin Luther King Jr. Memorial at night. They had planned to see others, but the temperature had dropped with the setting sun, so they decided to head home to do some studying and some work. Michelle had a final exam and final project for her Introduction to Public Relations class, so she needed the time to study, and Rashad always seemed to have work that he could do.

Michelle had packed a few things for overnight along with her book, notes and folder, and after Rashad let Shaka out into the yard for a few minutes, they hunkered down in the den, where Rashad could work on his computer and where Michelle could sit at the other desk.

They were actually productive for almost two hours, and then Michelle got distracted by the aroma of Rashad's cologne. She got up from her desk to stretch her legs and found them carrying her to Rashad's chair. Her body was itching for a caress. "Soon" had come.

Michelle kissed the back of Rashad's neck and felt his goose bumps rise. She kissed and licked her way to his ear, then ran her tongue along the outer shell before moving to the inner lobe. Rashad murmured.

Being with someone who was able to please her and who had taken his time with her had changed everything for Michelle. Knowing she could be pleased by him made her body start to tingle and yearn for that pleasure. Knowing she could be pleased by their lovemaking filled her with desire and released her inhibitions. Knowing she could be pleased by him made her want to please him even more.

She moved from the back of his chair to the side so that while she kissed his neck and ear, she could run her hand over his chest and down to his groin. She found and caressed that summit until it grazed her palm, until Rashad groaned and spread his knees for her touch, until his hard crest jutted out from his blue slacks.

She swiveled his chair toward her and claimed his lips. He reached for her, but she moved his hands back down to the arms of his chair. Then, with her mouth still locked on his, she stooped down between his knees, unbuttoning his shirt and spreading it open. When her lips hit his chest, he shuddered, and when she ran her tongue over his nipple, his head went back and his hands formed fists on the arms of his chair. His excitement was turning her on more and more.

As she ran her tongue over his chest, stopping to suck his nipples into her mouth, she unzipped his pants and dipped her hand inside. His hips thrust forward as she ran her fingers along his shaft. She pulled her lips from his and searched his back pocket for his wallet. When she found it, she took out a condom and opened it. Then she peeled back his briefs, released his sex and rolled the condom onto it in time to dip her head and capture it between her lips. Rashad groaned and buried his hands in her hair.

His sounds and movements and being in control of him this way was making her wet and needy. She toyed with his body with her mouth, with her tongue until he stopped her, suddenly pushing her back and pulling her upward.

"You can't do this to me," he said. "You're so beautiful, and it's been so long."

"It hasn't been that long—a couple of weeks, max," Michelle said.

Rashad was breathy. "A couple of weeks is long with you."

Michelle pushed Rashad back into the chair and took off her yellow, crochet-trimmed pullover, her black flats and her yellow jeans. Rashad watched her with passion in his eyes.

"You're beautiful."

Michelle couldn't help smiling.

In only her bra and panties, she sat down on his thigh, her legs between his knees, and she wrapped her arms around his neck to kiss him.

His one hand found her breast and stroked the crest, making her moan, and his other trailed up her leg to the center of her womanhood, making her shiver.

He stood, lifted her and carried her to his bed, where

he removed her remaining items of clothing as well as his own.

"Close your eyes," he said.

"What?"

"Close your eyes."

Michelle looked at him for a moment and then closed her eyes.

His mouth covered hers and opened hers, exploring it. She felt him next at her breasts; his hot tongue roused them to taut pinnacles. She felt him next on the top of her thigh, moving up her leg to her moist center. Then his mouth covered her womanhood, and a hot rush came over her. Her back arched off the bed, and a hand palmed her breast. He sucked gently on her sex until it throbbed heavily, until her thighs trembled, until she cried out in pleasure, until she thrust upward against his soft lips and piercing tongue. His mouth was driving her toward the edge, and she clung to his spread, wanting to go there. No one before him had ever taken her that far. No one had given her that much.

She gasped when he took his mouth away, and her eyes flew open.

"I'm sorry," he said. "But I want you so badly. Do you want me to—"

Michelle pulled Rashad up toward her, letting him cover her with his body—her lips, her chest, her thighs. His pulsing sex touched hers, setting her on fire. She moaned and drew him inside her—just at her very entrance. Feeling him there made her moan again. Her hips bucked involuntarily.

He was poised to enter her fully, but he stopped, letting her rotate onto him, letting her bring herself just over his crest and back. He must be able to tell that she liked that. She liked it enough to call his name and start to tremble.

"You are so beautiful," he said. "You have no idea what you do to me."

When he finally thrust inside her, it was in long, slow strides.

Michelle felt herself clamp down on his shaft. Her breath was coming out in short pants. Her body was being pulled toward unspeakable pleasure. She ground her hips against his onslaught and cried out in pleasure as waves of contractions rippled through her womanhood, dropping her over the edge.

Rashad pulled his mouth from hers and called her name, still striding within her as he lost control.

"You are so amazing," he said once he caught his breath.

"So are you," she answered.

He fell upon the bed beside her, and she curled around him. He pulled off the spent condom and took her in his arms. They felt like sanctuary.

They fell asleep in each other's arms, their naked bodies pressed together, her head cupped in the dip of his shoulder, her hand resting on his chest, his arm around her hip. Sometime later, he must have gotten up and pulled the covers from underneath them and covered them because when she awoke in the night, she was covered and warm, still sheltered in his arms.

When they woke in the morning, they showered together and made love again. Then they showered again and got dressed for the day. She petted Shaka while he made breakfast. They both couldn't stop smiling.

By the time Michelle got to Nigel and Regina's to pick up Andre, she was almost an hour late, and she hadn't stopped at the office supply store for the things she needed for her final project or the grocery store for the things she needed to finish the lasagna she'd started to make.

She and Andre ran errands, and she got home with enough time left to help Andre with his homework, lay out clothes for them and do some studying of her own.

She carried all the bags in at once, entered the code for

her alarm and went into the kitchen to put the cheese in the fridge. She came back into the living room to—

There he was, strolling toward her from her bedroom—Lucius.

"How did you get in here?"

He blocked her way to the bedroom, so she couldn't run in, lock the door and phone the police. But then Andre was still on the living room couch, and she wouldn't leave him behind. Lucius was too close for her to get to the alarm keypad, unless he was drunk. He reeked of alcohol, but his stance was firm. She couldn't tell. Damn him.

"Get out," she said, "before I call the police."

His hand came out from behind his back. He had her phone in it.

"You won't be calling anybody. Will you?" he said.

He started stepping toward her, but she didn't back away.

"Andre, stay right there on the couch."

"Yes, Mommy."

"You," she said to Lucius. "What do you want? Why are you here? You want to stop paying alimony? You want to get out of child support? What? What do you want?"

He was in front of her now, and he banged his fist into his palm in front of her face as he had done before. Michelle squinted so that she wouldn't cringe, and she didn't back away.

"You think you're as strong as me?" he asked. He was getting frustrated because she wasn't showing her fear. She felt it, but she was tired of hiding, of running away.

"You're nothing but a whore who's paid for," he said. "And I'm tired of paying. You can't keep my son from me, and you're not as strong as I am."

Lucius was yelling in her face, and when he was finished, he grabbed her shoulders and pushed her down. She fell backward onto the floor, the back of her head grazing the door of the front closet.

"Mommy, Mommy," Andre yelled and started to cry.

"Stay where you are," she said to him. "It takes a big man to knock down someone almost half his weight. Doesn't it, Lucius?"

She scrambled to her feet. She didn't know what she would do, but she was looking around for something to hit him with. There was nothing within reach.

He took another step toward her, and this time she stepped back.

Then there was a knock at the door. She looked toward it and then at Lucius. Then she dashed for the door.

He caught her by the waist and flung her to the floor, but she was up again, pummeling him with her fists. Lucius took her by the shoulders and pushed her down again, and this time he raised a hand to strike her. She scooted back on the floor, lifting her arm to protect herself and trying to get ready for whatever came next.

Her mind flashed to the night before, to the comfort of Rashad's arms, and she missed that sanctuary.

Chapter 16

Rashad had only planned to check on Michelle, but it was early enough that maybe he could take her and Andre to dinner. If not, he might be able to start the model plane with Andre and give Michelle time to study.

He didn't expect Andre to get the door. And it wasn't long before he realized that Andre was crying. Between his tears, he said something, but Rashad couldn't understand what it was. Something was wrong. The door only opened as far as the chain would let it go, and Andre wasn't big enough to reach the chain. He stood inside the apartment, crying loudly.

Rashad backed up and landed with all his weight against the door, shoulder first. The chain didn't break, but it was ripped out at the doorjamb, and the door flew open.

Inside, he saw what Andre was crying over. Michelle was on the floor, and a man squatted over her with an upraised palm.

"Oh, hell no," Rashad said, stepping past Andre and around the coffee table.

He caught the man's upraised arm and pulled him back from Michelle. This must be her ex, Lucius. He was toppled backward, landing on his rump. He sprawled awkwardly for a moment, enough time for Rashad to lift Michelle from the floor, stand her on her feet and usher her to the side.

"Get up and get out," he said to Lucius. "Or you'll have me to deal with."

Andre had run to his mother, and she scooped him into her arms and quieted him.

Lucius got up from the floor, and Rashad could see that this man had an inch or two on him in terms of height. Lucius also had more on Rashad in terms of weight; his shoulders squared off like a brick wall, and with such a bulky frame, he might have had seventy or seventy-five pounds on Rashad. Rashad didn't care.

"You're taking up for this whore?" Lucius said. "Maybe you don't know that I pay for her."

"Who," Rashad said, "are you calling a whore, and—"

"She knows who I'm talking about. That whore."

"Get out, Lucius," Michelle said. "Get out."

The alarm started to beep, and the phone that Lucius had placed in his back pocket started to ring. Lucius hurled it across the room, and it went dead.

Lucius took a menacing step toward Michelle with his fist balled, but Rashad stepped between them.

"No you won't," Rashad said. "Not while I'm here."

Lucius lunged at him, and Rashad put up his fists.

Then Michelle was at Rashad's side, holding his arm and shoulder.

"Don't," she said. "He's armed. He could hurt you."

"Bring it," Rashad said. "You may kill me, but that will get you life behind bars."

Rashad moved Michelle aside, but she got in front of him, between him and Lucius. Lucius grabbed her hair and yanked her backward, toppling her onto the floor.

That was it. Rashad was finished trying to get the man to leave. It was time for a good, old-fashioned whooping.

He stepped around Michelle and landed a punch on the side of Lucius's face. Lucius let Michelle's hair go and reeled sideways. When he regained his footing, Rashad was in front of him, leveling the next blow. Lucius stepped back, and Rashad stepped forward. Lucius stepped back again, and his back bumped the wall behind him. He turned his face to the side when Rashad neared, and he put his arms up in front of him, as if he were under arrest.

"Okay, okay."

Rashad backed off a bit but kept his eye on the other man.

"You hear that beep?" Rashad said. "How long you think it's been going? The police are already on their way. You just sit tight, and we'll see what happens next."

That was when Lucius drew the gun from the waist of his jeans.

"Oh, my God," Michelle said. She had gone to Andre, and when she saw the gun, she pushed Andre under the dining table and came back to Rashad's side. "Lucius, please don't do this. Don't hurt anyone."

Rashad was in front of him and stood his ground.

"I'm not scared of you. You think that's a toy? That's life behind bars."

Lucius started sidling away from Rashad and then started backing toward the door.

Rashad turned, watching Lucius as he backed away, watching him as he edged toward the door, watching him as he disappeared through the frame.

He went to the door and followed Lucius downstairs, keeping his distance.

"Don't go out there, Rashad," Michelle cautioned.

Lucius got into an old Ford pickup truck and tore out of the lot. Rashad ran outside but missed the license number in the dark.

He returned to Michelle, took her in his arms, brushed back her hair and squeezed her. Her shoulders had started to shake, and she clung to his neck, crying silently.

Andre had come out from under the table and was standing next to the counter dividing the kitchen from the living room with tears running down his face. Rashad motioned to him, and Andre ran over and hugged his legs. Rashad held Michelle with one arm and lifted the boy with the other and moved the three of them to the couch.

They remained there until the police arrived a few minutes later.

It was not unlike the last time, but they had a little more information to go on. They started canvassing the surrounding neighborhoods for the Ford pickup immediately, and since it was probably one of Lucius's vehicles from the construction company, they could have the Charleston police do some investigating to try to determine the license number. Rashad had also seen the gun. He didn't know guns, but it had a cylinder, so it was a revolver; it was small and had a black handle.

They both described the events they'd experienced, and Rashad was relieved to find out that Lucius hadn't had a chance to strike Michelle. He was disturbed, however, by the way she'd been handled. Given Lucius's size and girth, Rashad could see why anyone would be frightened and overcome. If Lucius wasn't so easily cowed, he probably could have even taken Rashad.

It had all happened quickly. They spent more time telling the police what happened than it had taken for the events to unfold. It took even longer for the detectives to collect prints.

"How did he get in?" an officer asked.

Rashad looked at Michelle.

"I don't know. The alarm was on when we came in, and I rearmed it before it went off. He was already here. He came from the bedroom."

"Do you mind if we check your apartment?"

"Not at all. Go ahead."

Rashad rubbed Michelle's shoulder. She had taken Andre onto her lap once her tears began to subside. He could see that both of them were still shaken and that Andre was groggy.

"You want to lie down for a little while before dinner?" Rashad asked, patting his head.

Andre nodded, and Rashad took him from Michelle's lap. The two put him in his bed and came back to the police.

"It was a window in the bedroom," an officer said. "It was broken into from the outside. He climbed through to get in without setting off the alarm."

"But I'm on the second floor," Michelle said.

"He must have used a ladder. Anything outside?" he asked another officer.

"No," the other officer said. "It's too dark to see markings, but he could have had a ladder in the truck."

Michelle put her face in her hands and shook her head. Tears stood out in her eyes but didn't fall. "I don't have an alarm in there. I didn't think of anyone getting in through a second-story window. I need a new alarm." She shook her head again and turned to Rashad. "I may need to relocate. If it's not here, it will be at my job, at Andre's school, when I'm at school, at my car before I get up here. How can I keep Andre safe?"

Rashad didn't like what he was hearing, but he understood Michelle's point, and he nodded his head in understanding.

"If we need to, we can move you to Baltimore. You can stay with my parents until you get settled. You can transfer your credits to Towson University and finish up there. I can come along once I get a job."

"Baltimore may not be far enough. What if Nigel and Regina drive up? All he has to do is follow them."

"We can make arrangements for that. We can be more careful. And right now, you're coming home with me."

"No, you've already done—"

"At least until you get a new alarm system or you find a new place."

"We'll stay with Nigel. He and Regina won't mind."

"If it helps," the detective said, "we have the make of his car now. Our chances of apprehending him just went up considerably. Either here or in Charleston, we're more likely to get him into custody."

"But when?"

Rashad heard the anguish in Michelle's voice and rubbed her back. He drew her closer and tipped his forehead to hers, stroking her cheek.

"It'll be okay. We'll figure this out. Hey, I'll stay on the couch tonight. You can pack bags for you and Andre, and tomorrow you can come over and stay with me or go stay with your cousin. Either way, I'm not letting you slip away from me."

"He could have—"

"But he didn't. Don't think 'what if.' And look, this man lacks the force of his convictions. He's not trying to use that gun or he would have. He'd rather intimidate you than fight with me."

Michelle shook her head, but she let it be.

After the police left, Rashad called a neighbor to let out Shaka, and Michelle finished the lasagna she'd started and woke up Andre. The three had dinner, and Rashad helped Andre with his numbers while Michelle studied. But it had gotten late, and the three didn't stay up long. Michelle packed bags for the next day, and they put Andre to bed. She fixed up the couch for Rashad and set an alarm clock. After she changed, though, she came to the couch to lie down with him, her back against his chest. She slept the night in his arms, their fingers intertwined.

In the narrow space of her couch, Rashad found that there was no place he would rather be. Inside him dwelled a tenderness that was almost painful. He kissed her hair and knew that he always wanted to keep her safe. He hoped she would come back to his house the next day, but he knew that either way, he wasn't letting her get away.

Chapter 17

Michelle finished counting out the registers at the coffeehouse and changed into her sweats to get ready for her class. This weekend she was only working the early morning shift to help out another manager. It would give her a couple of extra hours worth of money in her paycheck, and she had needed the same favor often enough. She called Mrs. Miller to check on Andre, and then she walked down Massachusetts Avenue toward the YMCA.

With classes and finals and final projects over, she had started a course in self-defense techniques. She needed to do something to feel more empowered; she couldn't hope that Rashad or anyone else would be there every time Lucius or some other threat appeared.

Her teacher was a kickboxer, and though she'd joined the class late, everyone made her feel at home. The class met twice a week, but this one had been moved to a Saturday because people were leaving for the holidays. The teacher took the center of the room.

"The tip for the day is to breathe and stay focused. Abdominal breathing can lower your heart rate to help you remain calmer so you can think. Okay. Last class we worked on two vital targets—the eyes and the nose. This time we work on two more vital targets—the neck and the knee. Everyone find a partner."

Michelle turned to the person closest to her and followed the teacher's instructions. She and Rashad had a date that afternoon, but Michelle couldn't forget the ever-present danger hanging over their heads. After what had happened last weekend—Lucius getting into her apartment through a second-story bedroom window—who knew what else he could do? He could still try to take Andre. And he might now want to hurt Rashad. He was also carrying a gun. No amount of bravado would overcome that if he became willing to use it.

She switched roles with her partner and followed the teacher's model. She thought of Lucius to work up the nerve to strike with all her might. A halfhearted effort wouldn't do, not if she was going to be prepared.

"That's it for the knife hand strike to the side of the throat," the teacher said. "Now we're going to use our elbows carried by the weight of our bodies. Watch while I demonstrate on the model."

Michelle watched the teacher and imitated her moves. The model was bigger than the instructor. Maybe this was something she could use on Lucius, who was bigger than she was. Little Andre had no defenses. She had to be his defense. She had taught Andre how to dial 911 and had taught him to yell "911" in an emergency.

Thinking of Andre reminded Michelle that she needed to decide on the options she'd come up with for his Christmas presents. It was almost Christmas, and his were the last presents she needed to get. She had gotten something for Rashad already. Andre's she couldn't hide as easily, and she needed to see what her budget would allow. They were going shopping today, with only days to spare, so she needed to make up her mind.

The class was now on the knee.

"I want you to do the move three times in rapid succession," the teacher said. "Keep going. Soon we're going to put some of these moves together—throat, eyes, knee. Think in threes. Rapid succession. Harder. Come on."

Even though she was still switching off with her partner, Michelle was getting tired. She would need to start building up her strength and endurance—both for the class and for real life. She felt her fortitude already being tested. A week had gone by since they had the make of Lucius's vehicle, and she was still waiting for them to catch him. It would give her back her life, if only for a little while and perhaps even longer.

At least she was in her own place again. She had stayed with Nigel and Regina for the first half of the week, but her new alarm was in now. That only protected her at home and, even then, only inside. She was carrying defensive spray everywhere else. That and looking over her shoulder all the time. That and second-guessing her decisions all the time. That and…

In the midst of her class, Michelle felt tears come to her eyes. She fought them back, trying to channel her feelings into the task at hand. She shook her head to clear it and refocused on her teacher.

"Now we're going to add the primal yell. Remember, get loud. This sends the signal for help, and it will ward off someone looking for an easy prey. Watch the move that I'm doing, and add the yell. Words like *no, don't, stop, police* and *911* work well. We're using the primal yell. Get loud."

Michelle hated the yell, and she wasn't good at it, which was why she needed this class. Rashad couldn't always be there to fight Lucius; she needed her own voice, her own formidable presence, her own yell. Her mind went to Rashad and the sight of him facing the gun held by Lucius, putting himself at even greater risk by standing up for her. The mess that she'd pulled him into was not only sizable, but also dangerous. She'd pulled him into her black hole.

"What if he has his arms around you like this?" another member of the class asked, demonstrating on her partner.

"That's a good question," the teacher said. "When we come back after the Christmas break, we do a brief review, and then we talk about getting out of common holds. Let's walk it out to cool down."

After class, Michelle picked up Andre from Mrs. Miller and went home. She showered and put on a pair of tights under a floral-print crinkle skirt. Then she added a pink sweater over her lace-trimmed blouse and finished off with her low boots.

When Rashad got there, she could see the neck of a black turtleneck under his overcoat. This was a little different for him; she'd only seen him in dress shirts before. Today he had on jeans and sneakers. She liked to see him a little more casual.

Michelle added a few extra things to her satchel to spend the night with Rashad, and the three headed out.

It was almost two o'clock by the time they got to the National Zoo, but they decided they could do just a couple of hours for their first visit. It was a bit chilly, so they decided to stick to the indoor exhibits as much as possible for this trip.

They parked at the lot near the Kids' Farm, where Andre got to pet some animals and got interested in rabbits. Then they took the main walk so that they could see the great cats, the Reptile Discovery Center and the invertebrates.

Rashad and Andre were fascinated by the animals, but Michelle was taken by their interaction with each other. The way Rashad cared for Andre and the way Andre looked up to Rashad touched her spirit. It also scared her. Who knew what would happen in their future? Mainly, though, it made her realize what she and Andre had been missing in their lives.

She had been quiet, thinking.

"Are you getting to know a little of the D.C. area?" Rashad asked her.

"We both are—Andre and I," Michelle answered. "I can't believe I've been living here as if none of this existed. Andre's been missing out. Thank you for showing it to us."

"One, stop thanking me. And two, Andre wasn't missing out—not on anything important. He had a mother working her butt off to make a good life for him and to keep him safe. He had your love."

They were still at the invertebrate exhibit, and Andre was looking at hissing roaches from Madagascar. Michelle made a face of disgust. She and Rashad both chuckled; then Rashad collected the little one on his hip. Andre rested his head on Rashad's shoulder and let himself be carried.

Their last stop was the Small Mammal House. They didn't get to the Amazonia exhibit so that Andre could see the tarantulas. Perhaps that was for the best. And they didn't make it to the Giant Panda Habitat. They would definitely have to come back, maybe over the summer when it was warmer.

Since they were near Rock Creek Park, they took a scenic drive and then stopped. Rashad had brought a soccer ball for them to kick around for a bit. There had been only two days of snow so far, and none lingered, so they could romp. Michelle played with them for a while but then sat out the second half; her boots weren't great for sports.

When it started to turn dusk, they dropped off Andre at Nigel and Regina's for the rest of the night. Michelle had been keeping him close, but she needed to get his Christmas present before it was too late.

"I've decided on a mini-laptop for Andre as the main thing. What do you think?"

"What else are you getting?"

"I want to get him military dog tags and a few of the toys he liked, maybe a couple new games for the portable game system, maybe a couple of DVDs and books."

"You don't need the games because he has the tablet. Everything else sounds good. The laptop will be useful if you get the right programs on it, especially with schoolwork as he gets older."

"What are the right programs?"

"Let's do this. You get the laptop, and I'll get and load the programs he needs. Deal?"

"You don't need to get him—"

"I want to do this. I know what he can use. Trust me. Deal?"

Michelle wavered for a moment, but she wanted what was best for Andre. "Okay."

"So," Rashad said, "we have a zillion places to get to and engraving to get done. Aren't you glad I'm driving?"

Michelle swatted his arm. "Don't start with me."

He leaned over and kissed her briefly on the lips. This never failed to send a pulse through her body, and when they pulled apart, she was holding her breath.

"Where first?"

"Mini-laptop first. That's the expensive thing. I'll know how much I have for other stuff after that."

"Okay."

Rashad took Michelle's hand, and they started on her Christmas shopping for Andre. When they were done a couple of hours later, they had everything but the dog tags, which would be ready in a couple of days. Rashad had the programs for the mini-laptop and would load them that night so that she could take it home and wrap it. The car was full of bags, most from the toy store.

"Where are you going to put all this so he doesn't see it?"

"After I wrap it tomorrow, I'll put it all in the living room around the little tree I have on the coffee table. He'll see them."

"And shake them," Rashad said.

"But he can't open them until Christmas."

"Which is less than a week away. I guess that's not too torturous."

They had dinner at Union Station to end the night.

"Why are you so quiet?" Rashad asked.

"Am I?" Michelle hadn't noticed. "I guess I've been thinking a lot."

"Lucius and all."

Michelle nodded. She didn't want to talk about it; she didn't want to bring them down. But maybe some things needed to be said.

"Rashad, I'm so sorry I dragged you into this mess. I don't want you to get more involved. Lucius could hurt you."

"Don't worry about me. Your job is to worry about Andre."

"I am worried about Andre. Every time Lucius has done something, he's told me I can't keep Andre from him. I don't know what I'd do if he got hold of Andre. He's not… he's not like you. He hasn't shown any real caring for his son."

"Or his wife," Rashad added.

"I'm not his wife anymore, but Andre—"

"Will always be his biological son."

"Yes, but that's not what I started out talking about. It was about you. I don't want you to get hurt trying to watch out for us."

"I won't. Lucius won't get Andre, either. And I want to be here to help look out."

Michelle shook her head. She had her doubts, and they

weren't going to agree on this. She didn't want her worries to overshadow their night, so she put them aside and tried to have a good time. That wasn't difficult with Rashad. They spent the rest of dinner talking about plans for the holidays and last-minute shopping needs, classes she'd be taking next term and projects he had lined up at work, what they might take at the Art League, how they spent the holidays as kids.

After dinner they went back to Rashad's place. Shaka met them at the door and kept them company while Rashad loaded the programs on the mini-laptop. When he was finished, Rashad went to let Shaka into the yard.

"Meet me in your room," Michelle said, grabbing her satchel. "I'll be a few minutes."

"Okay. I'll get us dessert."

Michelle smiled and went up to Rashad's room. Inside the bathroom, she freshened up and then pulled a white teddy and two-inch silver heels from her satchel. She took a breath and stripped down. She put up her hair with two silver combs, leaving curls coming down at her temples and ears, and she did her makeup. When the teddy was in place, she checked her face, slipped on the heels and sprayed her body with perfume. She should have brought a cover-up, but she hadn't thought of it.

When she was finished, she opened the bathroom door, exhaled slowly and stepped into the room.

Rashad was sitting on the edge of the bed next to his nightstand, which held two pieces of cheesecake and two glasses of wine on a wooden tray. He had the dim lights on and had taken off the vest he had worn over his turtleneck.

When he looked over and saw her, the passion that clouded his eyes rewarded Michelle for her effort, and she smiled.

He got up and crossed over to her, and she stepped into his embrace, reaching for him as he reached for her. He pulled her against his hard body, but his lips on hers were soft and gentle, his kiss searching and tender.

"Michelle," he said against her ear when they broke their kiss, "you look beautiful."

"Thank you," she answered, not knowing what else to say.

He stepped back to look at her, his hands on her hips turning her from side to side. Her breasts were swelling at the edges of the little teddy, and her nipples hardened under his gaze. He ran his knuckles over one, and she let out an involuntary murmur. In response he stooped and covered it with his mouth, sucking her through the silky swatch of fabric. She felt a heavy pulse building in her sex and moisture flowing to meet him. This man always turned her on.

She drew him up to her, took his face in her hands and kissed him again, pressing her body against his. She wanted to feel the sweet pressure of his body against her throbbing womanhood. In response, he cupped her buttocks through the teddy with both of his hands, lifted her against him and ground her along his center. Michelle could feel the ridge of his manhood grazing her sex through the thin mesh. She couldn't help moaning as the fire shot through her body. She couldn't help angling her hips to increase that sweet pressure.

"Rashad," she said, "you feel so good against me."

He kissed her eyelid and then her lips. He continued to grind her sex against his. He continued to make her moan.

When he set her down, they were both breathing heavily, but Michelle didn't want to stop. She moved her hand between them and touched the taut bulge in Rashad's jeans. His body jerked, and he looked at her, shaking his head.

"You have no idea what you do to me," he said.

Then he covered her lips with his and took a step back with her. When her back bumped the bedroom wall behind her, he stopped. He ground his body into her, then pulled back, stooping to take her breast into his mouth again. This time, however, he joined that pressure with his fingers between her thighs.

She was sure he could feel how wet she was through the fabric, but in moments she didn't care. With his mouth on her breast and his fingers kneading her sex, she was soon lost in the sensations coursing through her body. The need for fulfillment burned her like anguish. She called Rashad's name and thrust against his fingers.

When Rashad pushed aside the flimsy strip at the bottom of the teddy and dipped his fingers into her wetness, Michelle cried out and grabbed on to his shoulders. He was pushing her toward the brink, and her body thrust along that threshold.

Rashad pulled his mouth from her breast, and Michelle winced. Without thinking, just reacting, she covered her breasts with her own hands to caress the needy globes. Passion glazed over Rashad's eyes as he glanced at her, but he didn't return his lips. He knelt before her, drew his hand from between her thighs and covered her sex with his hot, wet tongue.

"Rashad," Michelle cried out as the fire from his mouth licked over her core.

The throbbing was building in her body, and she pushed along the source.

"Rashad," she cried out again as his hands reached up and covered her breasts.

"Rashad," she called as the spasms started inside her, making her hips push harder.

"Rashad," she called as an agonizing pleasure pulsed through her womanhood, dropping her over the edge.

She nearly collapsed on top of him when it was over. She couldn't catch her breath and couldn't steady herself against the wall.

His arms came around her, and he pulled her from the wall into a standing position, steadying her while she came back to herself.

He kissed her forehead and her lips and looked into her face.

"Are you all right?"

Michelle blushed under his gaze and nodded. She rested her head against his shoulder and let herself be held in the haven of his arms.

When she could breathe normally again, Michelle lifted her head and kissed Rashad's lips. No one had ever made her feel this way or this much, and she didn't know how to convey the feelings that inundated her. Being with this man let her reclaim her sensuality, let her experience her sexuality.

"Thank you," she said. "Thank you so much."

"One, stop thanking me. I loved doing that. And two, we're not done yet. Are we?"

Michelle ran her hand along the front of Rashad's jeans and felt his manhood.

"Not by far."

"Thank goodness," he said. "Because you've turned me on so much that I'm ready to explode." He laughed.

"I can fix that," she said.

Michelle took Rashad's hand and led him to the bed. He stopped at the dresser to get a condom and then followed her lead. She took his clothes off, kissing his body as it was revealed. The firmness of his chest and shoulders and thighs was making her feel sexy again, and when she rolled the condom onto him, she could feel her moisture flowing again.

She patted the bed for him to lie down and pressed his shoulders back, settling him onto the bed.

Then she climbed onto the bed, still wearing her heels, and straddled his thighs.

His back arched and his hips bucked as she began gyrating over his body. She bent down to kiss him briefly and then leaned up to rock up and down along his length. When she brushed her breasts across his chest, he murmured and twisted. She dragged herself down his torso to nibble at his nipples, and he groaned, thrusting upward.

His pleasure and the feel of his sex against hers had excited her again, and when she was ready, she unsnapped the crotch of her teddy and lowered herself onto him. He filled her with delight, and she felt him arching toward her in the midst of his own pleasure.

He reached up for her breasts, and she bent down for his lips. His hands grasped her hips and began moving her upon his sex. He called her name, and his thighs tensed. He called her name, and his thrusts became short and hard. He called her name, and his breaths became heavy and labored.

Her body tightened around his, and she felt the first waves of her release ripping through her. She moaned and rocked upon him.

His body tensed and began to shake, and he poured upward into her, all his pent-up desire thundering through him.

After their bodies calmed, Rashad removed the condom and covered them. Michelle spent the night in the harbor of his arms, their bodies pressed together, their fingers woven into one. How she adored this man.

Yet, being with her was exposing him to danger. The contradiction didn't escape her thoughts, not even as she began to drift. What they shared was something she'd only dreamed of, but it couldn't erase her past. Could it close that black hole? Could she?

Chapter 18

Rashad applied his Ferragamo pour Homme cologne and some lip balm and was finished in the bathroom. He wrapped a towel around his waist and padded into his room for clothes. Tonight was special, not only because it was just a couple of days until Christmas but also because he had made a decision, and he was acting on it tonight.

He took his two-button, navy Brooks Brothers suit out of the closet and laid it on the bed. It was his Madison Saxxon Herringbone 1818, and it was one of his best. He selected a striped Oxford button-down dress shirt to go with it and pulled an undershirt out of his dresser, along with a pair of boxer briefs and navy socks. He tossed those on his bed and started pulling on his underwear.

He was seeing Michelle tonight, and he wanted it to be special, as special as it had been when she'd stepped out of his bathroom in a white teddy and two-inch heels, as special as it was when she smiled at him. He wanted that smile around him every day.

Rashad buttoned up his shirt, stepped into his trousers and found his navy-and-black-checked tie. He put on the tie and sat down in his armchair to pull on his socks and his black calfskin wing tip shoes. He got his good black leather belt from the rack and threaded it through the hoops along his waist. He tossed the towel in the hamper and went to his dresser. Shaka had come in and now followed him, getting between his legs. He picked up his little Yorkie, rubbed his head and put him on the newly vacated armchair.

He'd been thinking more and more about it, more and more about her, more and more about them—Michelle and Andre. He loved the woman. There was no denying it. And he adored Andre. Everything in him wanted to protect them and keep them safe. This simple, unadulterated urge had overcome any hesitation he had had over getting serious with a woman, over committing to a relationship, over thinking about marriage.

Rashad emptied the dish he kept on his dresser into his palm and dropped the contents on his bed. He plopped down beside the little pile and put on his class ring, his gold tie clip, his curb link gold chain and his Invicta watch. The rest of the pile he scooped back up and returned to the dish.

Rashad took a final look in the mirror above his dresser, confident in his decision. He wanted Michelle to marry him, and he wanted to raise Andre as his own. She may have defied his initial expectations, but those had been long rewritten. She was the perfect fit.

On the nightstand next to his wallet sat a small black jewelry box. He grabbed them both and headed downstairs.

Shaka had yelped at his departure and then followed him downstairs. At the chime of the doorbell, Shaka bolted to the foyer. Rashad put the jewelry box in the candy dish on his end table; they would be going out first. He grabbed his overcoat and met Michelle at the door.

Michelle drove them to Georgetown, where they parked and walked to 1789, the restaurant Rashad had chosen.

Michelle took off her long winter coat. She had on a navy skirt suit. It fit close to her body and had a ruffle at the hem of the blazer that spread out over her hips. She had on black pumps and carried a black pocketbook. Her hair was pulled back in a tight bun at the nape of her neck, and she wore a string of blue pearls and blue pearl stud earrings. Her makeup was done to perfection, and the smile on her face set off everything else. She looked like every fantasy he had ever had.

Michelle ordered the lamb leg, and Rashad got the duck breast. They needed help with the wine selection but ended up with the perfect matches for their meals.

"If you're still going home for Christmas," Rashad said, "I need to give you your presents to take with you when we get home tonight—yours and Andre's."

"I'm not going home. I talked to my parents yesterday, and we all pretty much figure that Lucius will be back in Charleston for the holiday."

He covered her hand with his, and she linked their fingers.

"It's just best for me and Andre if we stay here," she said.

"Then come home with me to Baltimore. I want to be with you on Christmas, and Andre can meet my nieces and nephews. They'll have a great time together. We can stay over with my parents and unwrap presents in the morning. I would love for us to be together."

She hesitated.

"I already have plans to spend the day with Regina and Nigel. Let me check with them before I say yes. I don't want to be ungrateful to them. And we're family—they might have feelings about me ditching them on the holidays."

"Check with them, and if they have to have you there, then we can house hop. We can go to my parents tomorrow, open presents Christmas morning and both get to Nigel's in time for lunch or dinner."

Michelle smiled at that.

"Okay, let me check."

He loved her smile and couldn't help returning it, especially knowing that they would be with his family for Christmas. He had really wanted that.

He ran his fingers over hers, wondering if he should have brought the ring. He could have proposed at the restaurant. But then he wanted it to be a private moment. He wanted to be able to kiss her afterward, take her in his arms, make love to her. He wanted it to be…special.

After dinner they went to Blues Alley to listen to some jazz. It was two days until Christmas, so there were jazz arrangements of Christmas songs mixed in throughout the traditional jazz selections. Michelle watched the bandstand, but Rashad was looking at her. She was crazy gorgeous. He couldn't keep from touching her, even if it was just his palm to her back or his hand over hers. It was even better knowing that she was the one whose hand he would be touching for the rest of his life—he hoped.

They each had a glass of wine, and then they danced to a set.

"You know," Rashad said, "I have to find a club to take you to one day. I have to see the wild girl."

Michelle backed up from him, still holding his hand, and did a couple of club moves before cracking up. Rashad loved it.

"Yes," he said. "We're definitely going."

"Let's do a club for New Year's," she suggested. "I haven't been in forever, though, so be forewarned. I may embarrass you."

"Never."

"Aw," she said. She cupped his jaw and kissed him. "Thank you."

"You've got to stop thanking me."

"But I do. Look, I'm out in D.C. at a jazz club. I have a life. And I even know how to get here now."

They both laughed.

"You've given me a life, too," he said.

He was thinking that he wanted that life—his life with her—until the day he died. He didn't say that, but he sighed.

"See," she said. "See how sweet you are. Thank you."

"Stop it."

I love you, Rashad thought. But he only gazed into her eyes.

"Hey," Michelle said. "If I'm going to see your parents, I need to bring them something."

"No, you don't."

"Yes, I do. I'm from the South, and when we go visit people, we bring something. It's a sign you were raised well. What can I get them? Do they drink wine?"

"How about a bottle of champagne to usher in the New Year? We can stop on the way up."

"Perfect."

When the music turned slow, Michelle stepped toward him. Rashad took her in his arms, and her hands went to his shoulders. He felt proud to have her in his arms, blessed to have her gaze on his face. He was also excited to have her body sway against his. As she moved with him, he felt himself grow heady and hot.

She could probably see the passion in his face. He knew she could feel that he was becoming aroused. He stepped back to give her space, but she stepped toward him, bringing herself harder against him. She ran her cheek against his jaw and then closed her eyes and kissed his lips. Damn, this woman made him yearn.

He wanted her right then, wanted to toy with her until she was the one wanting to lose control, but he settled for the sweet agony she stirred inside him. He settled for the thought that tonight she really would be his. He hoped.

"I can't wait to make love to you," he whispered against her ear.

"Soon," she said, and they both smiled.

They walked the long way back to her car. Rashad needed the time to cool down a bit, and she seemed to want a stroll. They took in some of the shops along the main strip and then cut up toward the car.

Michelle drove them home, and Rashad let them in. He let Shaka out for a little while and then left him in the kitchen with a cluster of dog treats lining his dinner bowl. He came to the living room to find Michelle standing in front of one of his paintings.

He stepped up behind her, put his arms around her waist and kissed the side of her head. He wanted to run his hands down the front of her blazer and up the hem of her skirt, but he put such thoughts aside to focus on the moment at hand. This was one of the most important moments of his life, and he wanted it to be special.

"I need to talk to you," he said.

"Okay. Is everything all right?"

"Everything is perfect. Come sit on the couch."

Rashad guided Michelle to the couch, and when she had taken a seat, he took a breath, kneeled down in front of her on one knee and took one of her hands in one of his. He picked up the candy bowl from the end table and held it in front of her.

"Would you like a piece of candy?"

She shook her head. "I'm fine."

He smiled and held the bowl closer to her.

"Are you sure? They're chocolate, and one of them is calling your name."

She finally looked at the bowl. On top of the bed of Hershey's Kisses with Almonds wrapped in gold foil sat the black jewelry box.

"What's this?" she asked, picking out the box. "It's not Christmas yet."

He just smiled until she opened it. Inside she found a one-and-a-half-carat diamond solitaire set in fourteen-karat yellow gold.

Her mouth fell open, and she looked back at him.

"Michelle, I love you. You are exactly what I've always waited for. And I love Andre. I want to be there for both of you, protect both of you, be with both of you. I've never loved anyone this way—ever. I want Andre to be my son, and I want you to be my wife. And I can only promise that I'll never stop loving you, and I'll never stop wanting you, and I'll never stop trying to please you, and I'll never need anyone else. If you love me, please be my wife. Michelle Johns, will you marry me?"

Tears had come to Michelle's eyes as he spoke, and she clutched the box to her chest and squeezed his hand. Rashad held his breath and waited.

She didn't say anything for a long while. Then the tears that had welled up in her eyes dripped down. She started shaking her head.

"I can't.... We can't...." She was searching for words. "It would..."

"It would what, Michelle? Tell me."

"It would be a mess. It already is a mess. There's a maniac in my life who's already pointed a gun at you—a gun, Rashad. It wasn't a toy. We have to look over our shoulders constantly, wondering when he'll reappear, whether he'll try to take Andre, what he'll do next. This will hang over our heads like a guillotine, just as it does now."

"He'll be caught, Michelle. This is just temporary."

"This isn't going to go away. It might—for one year,

two years, three years. And eventually it starts all over again, probably with even more vengeance. It will always be nagging at us. I can't allow that."

"Let me help protect you, protect Andre, keep you both—"

"You can't be there all the time. Nobody can. And I can't let you think I'd marry you so that Andre and I can be protected or supported."

"Marry me because you love me. That's the only reason I'd want you to. Michelle—" he squeezed her hand "—do you love me? Are you in love with me?"

Another set of streaks joined the first set as fresh tears spilled down Michelle's face.

"That's not the point. In a way, that doesn't even matter. If I do love you, I shouldn't put you in even more danger than I've already put you in. If I do love you, I shouldn't drag you into this black hole with me."

"Your life isn't a black hole. And I love being with you. I love you."

"You're not getting it. Lucius could have blown off half your head, and I could be visiting you on the coma ward right now. I hate it. I hate that he's a constant threat to everything that I love, everything that makes me happy. But he is. He is."

"If that means that you love me, that I make you happy, then marry me. Don't let him win."

"I'm trying to be fair," she said. "And I'm trying to take control of my own life. I have to sort this out and resolve it *before* I try to build something new with someone else."

"What we have is already a structure. It's already furnished and ready to occupy. I would go anywhere we needed to go, do anything that needed—"

"The reason I didn't come back here after he broke in through the window, the reason I stayed with Nigel and Regina, the main reason—it's because I didn't want the situation with Lucius to force this relationship, to turn this into something it wasn't ready to be. Now I'm getting ready to go meet your parents again."

Rashad didn't know what else to say. His world seemed to be falling down, and no words he had seemed able to prop it back up.

"Okay," he conceded, shaking his head. "Let's take it slower then."

"There's more of a problem here," Michelle said. "I've sent mixed signals, and I need to stop. Until this is over, I can't be fully there for anyone, and that isn't fair to you." Michelle withdrew her hand from his and stood. She handed him the jewelry box she had been clutching to her chest. "I can't marry you, Rashad. I can't be your wife. And until I can give myself freely to another person, it's not fair for me to be with you, to confuse you. I can't see you anymore."

She ran to the door while he was trying to figure out how they had even come to the turn they had just taken.

"Michelle," he called and followed.

She was fumbling with his locks with tears pouring down her face.

"Michelle, wait."

She undid the last lock, and, without looking at him, she flew from the house.

He watched her get in her car and drive away, toppling the final pillars of his realm.

It was two days before Christmas, and his world had collapsed. *Great.* She didn't take his calls or return them, and he finally had to get her cousin's number from the directory and call him just to make sure that she was okay. He left a message for her to return his call, but of course, she didn't. Her presents and the things he had gotten for Andre sat piled on his dining table. Not even Andre would get to enjoy his things.

Rashad went up to Baltimore alone the next day. He hadn't told anyone about his proposal; he thought he would simply announce their engagement. Now there was nothing to tell, and it was easier not to say anything at all. But he couldn't stop from being notably down. Even his brothers took the hint and ribbed him less. And even playing with his nieces and nephews didn't ease the ache.

He called Michelle every day for the four days he was at home, but none of his messages were returned. Okay, she needed some time. He didn't want to give her time, but he would. How much time he would give her he didn't know, but when it was up, no man-made obstacle would stand in his way.

Chapter 19

Michelle took the present she had gotten for Rashad from the living room and put it under her bed. She couldn't stand to see it and be reminded that she wouldn't be spending Christmas with him and his family, wouldn't be seeing him at all.

It was early on Christmas morning, and she had a little time before waking Andre up to open presents, time before she would have to put on a happy face for her son and the world. In the meantime, she sat at the dining room table and covered her eyes with her hands to hold back the tears.

For the past two days, she'd been walking around in mourning, but she hadn't found a flaw in her reasoning. Being with her put Rashad in danger, and the threat of Lucius wasn't going away. It would hang over them like a hailstorm. That bastard was ruining her life, but it was up to her whether or not she'd take someone down with her. It felt like cutting off her own flesh, but it was the right thing. When she could see her way clear of this, then she could have the prize. And then she could be one, too.

That meant she was on her own.

Michelle got up and went into the kitchen. She did the dishes as quietly as she could and then started preparing the ham and the cobbler that she was bringing to Nigel and Regina's. She packed the presents she had gotten for them and for Sharon; she picked up the living room, and she sorted the laundry for washing the next day. Then she got dressed, put on some Christmas music and plugged in the little tree on the coffee table.

When she ran out of things to do, she woke up Andre.

"Hey, pumpkin. Are you going to sleep in all day? Merry Christmas." She sat on the bed and gave her son a long, warm hug. "Aren't you coming to open your presents?"

Andre bolted up and bounded for the living room. Michelle tried to smile.

In the living room, Michelle took a seat on the couch while Andre circled the presents on the coffee table.

"Which ones are mine, Mommy?"

"Give me that one near your hand, the one with the snowman paper on it. That's mine from Grandma and Grandpa."

Andre brought her the present and turned back to the table.

"The rest are for you. Go ahead. Open them."

Michelle turned the package in her hands, not wanting to open it. She tore the paper off anyway. It was a scarf, and wrapped in the scarf were a cuff bracelet, an inspirational desk calendar and a card with a check from her father.

"Look what Mommy got," she said to Andre, wrapping the scarf around her shoulders. She put on the cuff bracelet and held up her arm. She also held up the calendar. "This starts in January, so I'll open it later." She wasn't succeeding at being cheerful.

Luckily, Andre's attention was occupied. He was ripping open his presents and piling them next to him on the couch, saying what each one was as he went along.

"What's this one, Mommy?"

"That's a little computer just for you. You have to be very careful with it so you don't break it. Cousin Nigel and I can show you how to use it. We might need to get a little desk for you to put it on. Open the rest of your presents, and we can look at that one later. We'll bring it to Cousin Nigel's with us. Open those two. Those are from Grandma and Grandpa."

When all his presents were open and Andre had selected one to play with first, Michelle went into the kitchen and made him breakfast. She checked on the cobbler and took it out to cool. The ham needed more time.

She took Andre his breakfast in the living room, switched off the CD player and put on cartoons that Andre could watch while he ate and played.

In the afternoon, she made a few Christmas calls, let Andre speak to his grandparents and had him change. Then she packed his mini-laptop, the ham and cobbler and the presents they were bringing. First they stopped at Mrs. Miller's, and next they headed over to Nigel and Regina's.

Her cousin greeted her at the door with a hug and helped her with her packages.

"What size ham did you cook? This feels like it could feed an elephant."

"Elephants don't eat ham," she said.

"We don't know that," he countered. "Hey, cousin, I had a call for you—Rashad. He wanted to know how you're doing."

Michelle didn't want to give explanations. She wasn't prepared.

"Thanks. He likes to check on me with the whole Lucius situation going on. He must not have gotten me, so he called here. I'm sorry to be a bother."

"It's no problem. I like Rashad. It sounds like he's doing some good looking out. Call him if you haven't spoken to him since yesterday."

"I will," she said and was relieved that he left it at that.

"This is Andre's new mini-laptop. I was hoping you could help him learn how to use it."

"Sure. You want to look at it now, Andre?"

Andre nodded.

They set the mini-laptop up on the coffee table. Nigel took Andre onto his lap and showed him how to turn it on.

"Oh, man," Nigel said. "Look at all these programs. Half the desktop is filled with icons, and most of these he can use right now. This is great. How did you get all these?"

"Rashad put those on it." It hurt to say his name. "I have the disks at home."

"Well, this is one to grow on. He'll be using this through high school."

Regina came in from the next room with Sharon and headed into the kitchen. Michelle followed to help.

"Men and their toys," Regina whispered. "They're going to be at that all night."

When the table was set, they ate. Then they exchanged gifts with one another, and, as Regina predicted, the boys made quick work of the toys Nigel and Regina had gotten for Andre and went back to the laptop.

Michelle took Andre home just after nine so that she could put him to bed and get ready for work the next day. She was tired from the tension of having to hold herself together, and she went to sleep right after Andre. At least she had made it through that day.

The next few days were not such an easy matter. She

was back to work but had no other distraction at home. She had time for her mind to wander to Rashad, time to miss his arms, his face, his presence.

That weekend, her phone rang. No name showed up on the caller ID, but the area code was 843—Charleston. She'd been vigilant about checking the caller ID to avoid calls from Rashad as well as Lucius. Now she wondered who this could be and whether it could be her ex-husband.

She turned from the phone to let it ring. Then she turned back. She was tired of being afraid to answer her own phone, and she was more than tired of the havoc Lucius was causing in her life. She thought of the primal yell and the jab to the neck, and part of her even wished it was Lucius so that that she could tell him a word or two.

She got her wish.

"Hello, whore."

For a moment, she didn't know what to say. Then she was filled with a calm rage.

"Don't you dare call me whore, you two-timing, pigeon-hearted mongrel."

"As long as I pay for you—"

"You pay the alimony and child support you're supposed to pay. There's not enough money in the whole world for you to buy me. Get it straight."

He wasn't used to her talking back, and he didn't seem to like it.

"When I get there, I'm going to knock you down to the ground."

"You might try, but you won't succeed. I'm not scared of you anymore. Only a coward picks on someone half his size. And that's what you are—a coward."

"I'm coming to take care of you, and I'm coming to get my son."

Michelle banged her hand on the table.

"Oh, hell no. The day you put a hand on my son is the

day you lose a hand. You're unfit. Un-fit. He deserves better than you, and you won't be getting him or—"

"You think you can stop me? You've seen you can't stop me. I—"

"You aren't worth my time. And I'll have something waiting here for you when you get here, so if you think I can't stop you, you've got another guess coming. Uh-uh. You won't be throwing me on the ground anymore, you two-timing coward. I'm waiting for you this time. This time you're going to have to bring it, and you don't got it to bring."

"When I get my hands on you, you'll feel it."

Michelle had been getting louder and now reined in her voice. She didn't want Andre to hear this.

"You don't have the common sense of a dog. When the police get you, you'll see. I'm not the one who'll feel, you bastard. You're going to feel for all the wrong you've done to me."

"I'm not going to feel a thing but your head beneath my fist. When I'm done with you, you won't even recognize yourself."

She could tell he was getting flustered. His comebacks were slowing down, and he was sputtering his words. *Good.* She didn't care. He was ruining her life, and she was tired of it.

"You think I'm something for you to walk on. You're a toe rag. You're what was made to clean my feet."

"You can't even satisfy a man, and you think I'm—"

"You got it wrong, mister. You're the one who can't even satisfy a woman. You're so lacking in the bedroom that the women flee. You're so lacking in the bedroom that—"

"You want to play the dozens with me? I got a dozen for you—two fists and two feet. When I come for you, I'll show you who's lacking—"

"You are, Lucius. You're not a man. You're not even a boy. And you're not worth any more of my time."

Michelle clicked off the phone and caught herself as she was about to bang it down. Andre was asleep.

She cradled the phone and spun on her heels, her hands balled into fists. She was about to walk away when it occurred to her that she needed to call the police.

She called the police detective she had spoken to before. She didn't get him, but she reported the incident to the officer who answered, told him the number that Lucius had called from and left a message for the detective working on her case.

She checked on Andre, in case she had been too loud, but he was still asleep. She emailed her lawyer and then changed for bed.

Lucius would be more vengeful than ever, but she didn't care. She was tired of being cowed by him. She was tired of having him control her life. Tired of having him threaten her happiness. Tired of being backed to the wall. Tired of living with his black hole. When she saw him again, she would give him an elbow in the neck and see how big and bad he was then.

He might shoot her, but she'd go down leaving her mark on him. She had already drawn up papers making Nigel and Regina legal guardians of Andre should anything happen to her. She'd done that after moving to D.C. She had reached the point at which she didn't care, the point at which she'd had enough, the point at which she was dangerous.

Michelle checked her thoughts. She couldn't be a danger in comparison to Lucius. He could beat her to death if he got the gumption. At least Rashad was out of the range of fire. Now she was going to stand up for herself. She was going to her gym class tomorrow. She would at least go out with a primal yell.

They knew he was in Charleston now. They had the number he had called from. They had the make of his car. Something was going to yield. It had to.

When she woke up the next morning, Michelle was still depressed and still angry. She dropped off Andre at Mrs. Miller's and went to work. She would have to be even more vigilant now. If Lucius wanted revenge, he could target Andre to hurt her, and given the man that he was, he might do just that.

Michelle was on watch that day and the next. That afternoon, though, she got glorious news. Her phone rang when she was at work. Usually, she wouldn't take it, but something told her to get that call. She grabbed her phone and took a seat at an empty table.

"Hey, Mom. I'm at work. I can't talk long."

"Oh, honey. They got him. I just heard from his mother. They arrested Lucius last night down here in Charleston. Seems he was in some kind of brawl at a nightclub. His mother's just beside herself because he's been getting himself into so much trouble."

"They arrested him?" Tears of relief formed in Michelle's eyes.

"Yes, siree. He's in jail right now. He won't be bothering you on the phone for a while. I'm so sorry I gave his mother your number."

"Mom, I have to go. I'll call you later."

Michelle found the number and called the police detective. She told him that Lucius had been arrested in Charleston and asked him what to do to get the other charges added. The detective said that Lucius should have been flagged automatically but that he would follow up on it. Her next call was to her lawyer. She was in court, but Michelle left a message.

Michelle sat back and took a breath. Lucius may not be

put away for long, but she would at least have a moment of serenity, a moment when she didn't have to look over her shoulder, a moment without the threat of him snatching Andre, a moment without having to think of him at all.

Michelle went back to work, but as her mind cleared of worry over Lucius, it turned more and more to thoughts of Rashad and the decision she had made. It had been motivated entirely by Lucius, and now that the threat of Lucius was gone, even if it was only temporary, she could think about it in a different way. With Lucius in jail, she could see that she had been letting him control her life, letting him make her feel unworthy of someone else, someone good.

Michelle counted out the register at the end of her shift and then changed into her sweats. She had an hour until her class, with no homework to read, nothing to do, so she sat down in the coffeehouse and sipped on a medium roast.

She hadn't seen or spoken to Rashad since she'd turned down his proposal just over a week ago. That was just before Christmas, and now it was New Year's Eve. Rashad had told her not to let Lucius win. She had been doing exactly that. He won when he controlled her decisions. He won when he kept her afraid. He won when she was forced to cut off her own flesh to keep it safe from him. He won when she was the victim.

Michelle didn't know what do to. Lucius would be out of jail at some point, and the threat would be there again. How could she keep him from winning in the long term?

When it was time, Michelle said goodbye to her coworkers and headed to her class. Afterward, she picked up Andre and took him home to get him dinner. All the while she troubled over what to do.

Andre was in the living room playing with one of the games she'd gotten him for Christmas when Michelle went into her bedroom to make the call. She got Rashad's

Christmas present from under her bed and dialed his number, knowing only that she had to see him.

"Michelle? Is everything okay?"

"Yes."

"You haven't returned my calls," he said.

"I'm sorry. I don't have an excuse. I've missed you so much."

"I've missed you more," he said softly.

"I'm sorry I made one big old mess. Can we talk?"

"I'd like that."

"Can you come over?" she asked.

"I'm in Baltimore. My parents had us all come up for New Year's Eve."

"Can I come up? I don't have to stay. I—"

"Come and spend the night."

"Can I bring Andre?"

"You have to bring Andre," he said and gave her the address. "Can you find it all right?"

The humor hung between them, but neither entered into it.

"I'll find it," she said. "I'll be able to leave in about an hour. I'll see you in two."

She hung up. She called and found someone who could cover her shift at work the next day. Then she searched through her closet, jumped in the shower and put on the dress she'd worn to Nigel and Regina's wedding. It was an orchid-purple knee-length gown, sleeveless with beadwork over the front. The gown had a solid shell but a sheer outer fabric, and the matching jacket had beadwork and sheer arms. When her face was done, she put up her hair, put on her two-inch black pumps and called Andre.

She pulled out a pair of blue slacks and a blue dress shirt for Andre, and while he changed, she told him where they were going and started packing overnight bags for them. She got on the computer for the directions to Baltimore and to the house. Then she stopped in Greenbelt for some champagne, and they got on the highway.

She got lost only once, and then they found the address they were looking for. She recognized the house from their last visit. She parked, took a breath, gathered their things and held Andre's hand on the way in.

Rashad's father answered the door and ushered them inside. She gave him the champagne, and he took the overnight bags from her. Rashad's mother came over to get their coats. Michelle recognized Rashad's brothers and in-laws from the Kennedy Center, and she smiled and nodded at them and the gathering.

Shaka found them before Rashad did, and he was leaping at her legs when Rashad came into the living room. Andre pulled free from her hand and ran to Rashad when he saw Rashad. Rashad caught Andre in open arms. He lifted the boy for a hug and then settled him on his hip.

Rashad set Andre down and stepped to her, taking her into his embrace as she wrapped her arms around his neck. They clamped on to each other in the same moment, and the tears that had already started to form in Michelle's eyes began to fall. She hadn't known she would do that.

He cupped her face with both hands and kissed her. Then he returned his arms around her and held her to his body again.

"God, girl, I've missed you."

"I've missed you, too."

They just held one another. Michelle could only imagine the spectacle they formed, and she stepped from him, blotting her eyes and trying to smile. She still had a gift bag in her hand, and she held it out to him.

"This is for you from us."

Rashad put his hand on Andre's head and tugged Andre toward him.

"You guys come open your presents, too," he said to

her. He put his arm around her and started drawing her through the room. "Everybody, this is Michelle. Michelle, this is everybody." People chuckled. Rashad lifted Andre again. "We'll be right back," he said to the room. "It's time for Christmas presents."

Inside his room at his parents' house, Rashad's bed was covered with presents.

"This is too much," Michelle said. "Why are they here?"

"I had them in my car. I started to bring them to you a thousand times, but you wouldn't answer my calls."

Andre had already climbed on the bed and was touching the boxes. Rashad rounded the bed and started handing Andre his presents. Then he sat in his armchair and took Michelle onto his lap so they could see Andre open up his gifts. Andre got two of the toys he'd been looking at in the toy store, a couple more programs for his new minilaptop and a little watch. He immediately started playing with the remote control car.

Rashad lifted Michelle from his lap and set her on the bed.

"The rest are for you."

Michelle started unwrapping boxes. He'd gotten her a gold heart pendant and chain similar to the one she'd picked for his mother. He'd also gotten her a gorgeous purple cocktail dress. She held it up to her body, stunned. There was a gift certificate to an art supply store taped to a box of chocolates with nuts. The last one was a GPS navigation system for her car. She swatted his arm but was genuinely touched by everything.

"It's too much, Rashad."

"Not for you. I love you."

"I love you, too."

He gathered her next to him and kissed her gently. When he pulled back, his eyes were glistening and a grin covered his face.

"I've been waiting to hear you say that," he said.

"You haven't opened your present," Michelle said. "Andre, come see Rashad open his present from us."

Rashad pulled the rectangular box from the gift bag and opened it. It was a large-link, stainless-steel ID bracelet like the gold one he'd gotten his father. The top read "Rashad Brown," and the other side was engraved, "With All Our Love, Michelle and Andre."

Rashad hugged Andre and kissed her, clearly moved.

"I know we need to talk," Rashad said.

Michelle looked at Andre. "It can wait. Let's spend time with your family."

"Are you sure? If we go back out there, we can forget it."

"I'm sure."

Rashad took them back downstairs and then down to a second living room in the basement, where the kids were. There he introduced Andre and Michelle to all his nieces and nephews. Andre had brought his remote control car down, and he and the two others his age started to take turns with it.

In the living room, Michelle and Rashad took a corner of the couch and started to chat with Rashad's brothers and his in-laws and his parents and some of the other guests.

"He got me a GPS navigation system," Michelle announced to his brothers, who laughed.

"Didn't I tell you not to keep ribbing this woman?" Derrick said.

"But she has no direction. Okay, did you get lost on the way here?"

"Only once," she said, and he laughed.

"What kind of present is a GPS?" one of his sisters-in-law said. "We have to school you on what to get for a woman."

"But he also got me this," Michelle said, fingering the heart pendant around her neck. "And a dress."

"Aw," all the women said.

Marcus and Keith gave Rashad the thumbs-up signal, but he waved them away.

"I taught you right," his father said.

"And what did you get me?" his mother countered. "An electric floor cleaner and a wireless television transmitter."

Everyone laughed, and Keith literally rolled on the floor.

"Wait here," his father said. "You put it down, and it cleans the floor for you. . . ."

Everyone laughed more.

"But he also got me this," Rashad's mother said, holding up her wrist and pointing to a gold watch.

"Aw," the women said again.

"See," Trevor said. "It's a confederacy of women. They're all in league."

"Hold up," Michelle said. "Wait till someone gets *you* a vacuum for Christmas."

The women laughed.

"I tell you," Rashad's father said, "it's not a vacuum. Keith, go get the thing."

Rashad kept his arm around her for most of the night, kissing her often. Around ten o'clock, Rashad pulled Andre onto his lap, where he fell asleep. Michelle caught Rashad's brothers exchanging glances with him, but she missed the full context.

"You want me to take him?" she asked, petting Andre's head.

"Nope."

"Are they teasing you about us?" she asked. "If so, all you have to do is let me know, and I'll give them a good talking-to and a swift kick in the pants, if needed."

Rashad laughed out loud and then kissed her gently. Michelle turned her head from the kiss in time to see two of Rashad's brothers exchanging a high five.

When she turned back to Rashad, though, he was looking at her and smiling.

"Pay them no mind," he said. "They're just acting Andre's age. And here I am, the youngest."

Michelle and Rashad put Andre down in the children's room, and the parents of the other little ones followed suit. Then Marcus accused Rashad of monopolizing Michelle, and Rashad's two sisters-in-law drew her into the kitchen, where they started cleaning up and chatting.

At almost midnight, all the adults gathered in the living room with glasses of champagne, and Rashad claimed her with his arm again. They put on the television to watch the ball drop in Times Square, and when the countdown ran out, Rashad took her into his arms and kissed her. She held his shoulders and kissed him back—a long, passionate kiss.

"Happy New Year," he said when they broke the kiss. He still held her in his arms.

"Happy New Year," she said back, and she thought it would be.

Chapter 20

Michelle checked the keyhole and opened the door to Rashad with a kiss. He held Shaka in one arm, and the Yorkie began scrambling to get to her. Michelle petted his head briefly and then went to the keypad to reset her alarm.

With the door closed, Rashad let Shaka down to the floor. He rushed to the couch, where Andre was sleeping, and jumped up on the nearest cushion.

"Shaka," Rashad said, "come down. Down, boy. Don't wake up Andre."

Shaka padded his way up Andre's body until he could lick Andre's face. Andre woke up with a squeal and started laughing.

"It's time for dinner," Michelle said, "so that's perfect timing."

"I hope it's all right that I brought him," Rashad said to Michelle. "He was getting tired being left home alone so often."

"We don't mind at all."

Michelle moved toward the kitchen, and Rashad followed.

"Let me help," he said.

"You can help with the dishes later."

"I can help set the table now."

"Okay," she said. "Where are the plates?"

"That I don't know."

Michelle started to chuckle.

"But you can tell me."

When they got the table set, with a bowl on the floor for Shaka, they called Andre and sat down to eat.

"How was your first day of classes yesterday?" Rashad asked Michelle.

"It was too soon. I have homework already. I can't believe Howard opens so early after the winter holidays. It was only New Year's a week ago."

"What are you taking this semester?"

"I have College Algebra I, Advertising Sales and Ad Copywriting and Design. I've already had most of the second-semester junior year classes, so after next semester, I'll be a senior. Hey, what are we taking at the Art League? That starts soon, too."

"What I really want is Apps for Artists," Rashad said.

"Me, too. Let's take that one. Oh, but I would need an iPad, right?"

"It's not offered until April, so you have time to get one. When's your birthday?"

"Don't even think about it," Michelle said. "You've done too much already."

"Well, while we're waiting for Apps, how about we take Basic Drawing together?"

"Okay," Michelle said. "But they have a zillion sections of that. Let's get in the same one."

"That's the plan."

After dinner, they did the dishes together. Then Rashad

played with Andre on his mini-laptop while Michelle read awhile for her classes. At eight-thirty, Michelle announced that it was time for Andre to get ready for bed. Rashad stayed while Michelle read Andre a story, and then they tucked him in, leaving Shaka at the foot of his bed.

Back in the living room, Michelle became serious.

"I have something to tell you."

"What is it? Is something wrong?"

They sat on the couch together, Rashad's arm going around Michelle's shoulder and her hand finding his.

"I got a call from my lawyer earlier today," Michelle said. "Lucius is out on bail."

"How did he get bail?"

"Exactly. How did he get bail in the first place, and how did he make bail in the second place? Maybe because he owns a business and is therefore seen as having ties to the community, but it still doesn't make sense."

"You might need a new lawyer," Rashad said.

"No, I don't think that's the issue. Don't forget that the lawyer for the bar brawl was there, too. Anyway, I don't want to worry you. I just wanted you to know."

"We have to be extra vigilant for a little while. Do you want me to stay tonight? I can get up early in the morning and make it to work."

"No, that's okay. You hadn't planned on staying, and we'll be okay."

"I don't mind taking the couch."

"I know, but we're fine."

"What about us?" Rashad took her face in his palms and drew her close to him for a kiss. "Does this change anything for us?"

Michelle shook her head. "No," she said. "I won't let that ruin things for us again."

He kissed her lips, and she smiled.

"Good because I've started making plans for us for this weekend."

"I'm in."

Michelle brought her arms up around Rashad's neck and kissed him. It was gentle at first, then passionate. They hadn't made love since before she had turned down his proposal, and the desire hung between them—thick and rich, palpable to the touch.

When they broke their kiss, Rashad looked at Michelle and sighed heavily. "I better get going," he said, "or I won't be going at all."

"I wish you could stay," Michelle said. "But you better go."

"I know."

"Soon," she said.

"Soon."

Rashad collected Shaka, kissed Michelle at the door and headed home. He couldn't wait until "soon" but settled with making their plans for Saturday. He had made their reservations and had picked out one of his good suits, and now he was counting the days.

When Rashad picked Michelle up from Nigel and Regina's, she was wearing a long teal skirt that flared below her knees, with a matching shirt and jacket. The jacket flared below her elbows, mirroring the skirt, and it hugged her waist like the skirt did, giving her that tall, hourglass shape. The material had a shine to it, and she had on her black pumps with it. Her hair was up, and she looked… stunning.

"Hi, beautiful."

Michelle had wanted that reaction, but now that she had it, she felt a bit flushed.

"Are you going to be warm enough in that?" Rashad asked.

"Are we spending a lot of time outside?"

"No, we're not."

"Then I'll be fine," Michelle said. "I have on tights, and I have my coat."

She gestured to Andre, who came to her open arms.

"Be good for Cousin Nigel and Regina."

He nodded vigorously. "You look pretty," he said to his mother. Then he turned to Rashad. "Can I come, too?"

Rashad rubbed Andre's head. "Next time, sweet pea. You figure out what we're doing tomorrow. Okay?"

"Okay."

At the door, Regina and Michelle hugged goodbye.

"You kids have fun," Nigel said.

Rashad took Michelle's overnight bag and put his arm around her as they walked to his car.

"So where to?" Michelle asked.

"I hope you feel like Italian."

Michelle nodded.

"Good. We have reservations."

Rashad drove them to Maggiano's in Chevy Chase. They ordered appetizers and let their waiter select wine to go with their veal dishes. Then they ordered a slice of cheesecake to share and talked about their weeks. Afterward, they were going to listen to some music, but as they stepped into the street, they were surrounded by the falling flakes of what was only the third real snow of the season. It was beginning to blanket the sidewalks and roads.

"Maybe we should head home early," Michelle suggested.

"I think you're right," Rashad said. "It seems to be sticking."

Back at his place, Rashad took Michelle's coat, and she went into the kitchen to let Shaka out into the backyard. Shaka didn't take very long, but when Michelle got back to the living room, the lights were off and Rashad had a fire going in the fireplace. A faux fur throw was spread in front of it with two wine glasses and an open bottle of merlot beside it.

Michelle moved toward the throw.

"Wait," Rashad said. "Come sit for a moment."

Rashad took a breath as Michelle sat down, crossing one leg underneath her. Michelle saw him kneel in front of her on one knee, and she knew what was about to happen. Then Rashad took the black jewelry box from his back pocket.

"If this is too soon," Rashad said, "you can say."

Michelle shook her head. "No, it's not." Tears were already coming to her eyes.

"I love you, Michelle."

"I love you, too, Rashad."

Rashad opened the box, and Michelle took the ring out.

"Please marry me. I'll always cherish you, and I'll love Andre as my very own, and I'll—"

Michelle felt her heart about to burst. "Yes, I will."

Rashad leaned up as she leaned down, their lips meeting and claiming each other. Rashad smiled as their kiss broke. Their arms remained around each other.

"I had a whole spiel ready," he said and then chuckled.

"Save it for your vows."

"I will."

They stood together and moved to the throw, where Shaka had taken a center seat. After they wrapped their arms around one another in front of the fire, Michelle's lips found Rashad's neck, and his hands slipped inside her jacket to her breasts.

"We haven't poured the wine," he said.

"There's time," she answered.

"Hey," he said, while he could still think, "we should plan an engagement party."

"You want to make sure I don't back out?" Michelle asked.

"Or let my brothers get their ribbing over with all at once?" Rashad added. "No, I want to let the world know that this beautiful woman has said she'll marry me."

"Let's tell Andre first—tomorrow."

"Will he be okay with it?"

"He'll be more than okay. He'll love having you as his father."

"I'll love having him as my son and you as my wife, and I'll—"

Michelle put her fingers to his lips and covered his neck with her mouth, taking his blazer from his shoulders.

Tonight, they were celebrating.

They told Andre the next day when they got to Nigel and Regina's. Everyone was gathered in the living room. Michelle and Rashad settled on the love seat across from Nigel and Regina, who held little Sharon. Michelle was wearing a red turtleneck with a matching sweater and black jeans, and Rashad had on a blue cardigan over a white shirt with blue jeans and sneakers. Neither one could stop smiling. Andre was still in his pajamas, and Michelle took him onto her lap so that she and Rashad could tell him that they were getting married.

"You're going to be my new daddy?"

"Only if you want me to be."

Andre nodded and hugged Rashad. Both Rashad and Michelle had to hold back their tears.

And since Nigel and Regina knew, Michelle had to call her parents. Rashad also called his family. His parents would tell his brothers, so there was no need to worry there.

They went to lunch with Nigel, Regina, Andre and Sharon. Then Andre, who got to pick their activity for the afternoon, wanted to go to the Smithsonian's National Museum of Natural History to see the dinosaur bones.

They did that, and they saw the exhibits on ancient Egypt and the Hall of Bones, as well. Rashad made them dinner at Michelle's place and left them on Sunday night. They both thought that there was still so much that they had to discuss.

The two didn't have time alone again until Wednesday evening, when Mrs. Miller was watching Andre. Michelle went to Rashad's for dinner after her last class let out, and they arrived at his house at the same time. Michelle called to check on Andre, and then the two began dinner—boiled tilapia fillets with wild rice and asparagus.

"So, do you think you'll like living here? At least until we find something better? We can outfit the spare bedroom for Andre, and we can fix up the den so that we can both share it. I'll have to stop letting Shaka use the yard as his bathroom so that Andre can play outside."

"I was wondering about that," Michelle said. "Don't you ever use it?"

"Now and then in the summer. But I'm building a barbecue pit, so maybe we'll use it more."

"We'll be fine here, and I can help pay the mortgage." Michelle saw that Rashad was already shaking his head. "It won't be a lot, but I can do my part, and don't even think about trying to stop me."

Rashad took Michelle's shoulders so they could face each other.

"How about you put all of that toward finishing school? Go full-time for your last year. And you won't be getting alimony after we're married, but I have enough for both of us." He could tell she was about to protest. "Just think about it for a bit."

"All right, I need to think through this and do a budget and—"

Michelle's phone rang. She fished in her purse on the kitchen table and saw that it was her mother.

"Let me get this. It's my mother."

Rashad nodded, and Michelle turned her attention to the phone. Their conversation was brief, and Michelle's mom did most of the talking. When it was over, Michelle stood frozen for a moment, her hands pressed to her chest. Then tears started streaking down her face.

"What is it?" Rashad asked, coming to her.

"Lucius is dead. Apparently, while he was out on bail, he was harassing another woman in Charleston. Her boyfriend killed him in her apartment."

Everything was done cooking, so Rashad turned off the stove and came back to Michelle, wrapping his arms around her.

"It's okay, honey."

"I'm not upset," Michelle said. "I pity him, but I'm also…relieved."

Rashad held her while her tears subsided. Then her head jerked up from his shoulder.

"I'm going to testify at the trial," Michelle said. "The one for the man who killed Lucius."

"They'll have all the information from the arrest warrants."

"I know. I'm going to testify anyway. And if there's anything left from his company, I'm going to split it between his mother and Andre's college fund."

"If he didn't have a will."

"Yes. But he probably didn't. He thought he was invincible. And he was so young."

"I know."

"I didn't want it to be over this way, but I'm…"

"You're glad that it is."

She nodded as fresh tears fell.

Michelle wrapped her arms around Rashad's neck and let her tears fall. No more looking over her shoulder, no more fear of what could happen to Andre or Rashad at

Lucius's hands, no more black hole. If only it could have ended some other way.

Michelle's tears soaked through the shoulder of Rashad's shirt. This was the woman he loved, and any pain inside her tore through him. He wanted nothing more than to ease those tears. He ran his hands along her back, holding her to him. Then he shifted her face toward his and kissed the wet prints etched there.

The feel of his hand at her back had already sent a tingle up Michelle's spine, and after Rashad kissed her cheeks, Michelle took his lips with hers, yearning for the comfort of their love. Rashad's lips opened her mouth to his searching tongue, raking her body with desire. He grasped her hips, lifting her against him.

Rashad felt Michelle's center settle against his and make him taut. He brushed her wet cheek with his thumb, filled once again with a tenderness that only this woman made him feel. He kneaded her buttocks through her sweatpants and then brought one hand up to her breast. He could feel how much she craved to be near him, how much she needed this release.

He stepped from her and took her hand, leading them upstairs.

Inside his room, he pulled her to him, wanting to show her that his arms were there for her and wanting to show her how much he loved and wanted her.

Michelle rushed into Rashad's arms. If felt like heaven. They moved at the same time, their lips finding each other's lips and their tongues exploring each other's mouths. They claimed each other with gestures of love.

Rashad slipped his hand between them and into Michelle's sweatpants to play over her womanhood with his fingers. He touched her wetness through her panties, which made her moan. He tugged aside the thin weave and caressed Michelle's moist flesh, finding her swollen pinnacle.

Michelle spread her legs, wanting that supple touch. She felt herself throb with sweet agony and couldn't stop the quick intake of her breath or the low moan that followed it. His touch obliterated her thoughts, filling her with pure sensation as it drove away the pain, the pretense, the past.

Michelle touched the hard wall of Rashad's chest, wanting his thick arms around her. She let her hand sink to his groin and felt him leap against her fingertips. Every flux of her fingers sent a current through his body, making him twinge like he was being raked on an electric carpet. He wanted that touch on his skin; he needed to feel her hands upon his flesh, her body against his.

They stepped back and discarded their clothes, and Rashad went to his dresser. He had a condom on when he met her on the bed. They moved for each other at the same time, a raw need building between them.

Michelle drew Rashad over her, and Rashad settled himself between her thighs, entering her in one fluid movement. Michelle arched her back until her breasts reached Rashad's chest. It sent a hot pulse through them both, and they began to toil together, loving the hurt away, loving the past away, loving each other.

When Michelle cried out his name, Rashad bucked inside her and had to fight to keep himself contained. He tilted his hips, letting her sex ride along his lower abdomen and his chest grate against her breasts as he spun inside her.

Michelle called out his name again, feeling herself tightening around his manhood as waves of contractions moved through her, pushing her over the edge. Rashad felt her grip on to his sex and couldn't stifle his groan. He felt her go taut and couldn't help wincing and bucking inside her as her waves passed over him. He couldn't help losing control.

Michelle and Rashad held one another in the sanctuary they had created between themselves. As their breathing and pulses slowed, their bodies knitted together, a shield against anything that would try to put them in jeopardy, an armor against anyone who would try to tear them apart.

After they showered and dressed, Michelle and Rashad packed dinner and collected Andre from Mrs. Miller to take him home. They ate together at Michelle's dining table. Then Rashad popped in the movie that Andre had picked—*Finding Nemo.*

"Are you sure you want to see this *again?*" Michelle asked.

"Yes, yes, yes." Andre jumped up and down.

"Yes it is," Rashad said, scooping him up and onto the couch.

Michelle joined them with a blanket and a tub of popcorn.

With Andre between them and their future together before them, Michelle and Rashad linked their hands, and the three of them cuddled up on the couch to watch the movie, now a family.

* * * * *